GRIMY, SHE WAS MY BEST FRIEND:

DEJA AND ONAH

RUBY

1

DEJA

I dreaded the whole day. My mother never came home the night before, and I got woken out of my sleep because someone was banging on the door like they were crazy. We lived in a three-bedroom townhouse in the Black Hills, and I hated living here. I got up from the bed, looking over at my baby sister, making sure she was still sleeping. I was twenty years old, still sharing a room with my little sister. The knocking continued. I popped my head into the boy's room, checking on my little brothers Zayden and Zyier before heading downstairs.

Knock! Knock! Knock!

"WHO IS IT?" I YELLED, THEN SNATCHED THE DOOR OPEN,

coming face to face with the leasing office lady and the maintenance men.

It was too early I wasn't in the mood to be deal with muthafuckas. I rolled my eyes at her. I know she was here being nosey.

She cleared her throat. "Is your mother home, it's a must I speak to her regarding her unit."

"Nah, she not home right now; what can I help you with?" I asked, folding my arms, waiting on to explain her surprise visit this early in the morning. She handed me a white envelope then turned around to walk off when I opened it, noticing it was a notice to pay one thousand for rent not being paid. I shook my head. My mom was reckless as fuck, and not paying the rent meant she hadn't paid rent in three months. On top of the court fees, she didn't have her job anymore, so that meant I had to step up and make sure we didn't get put out.

I walked back into the house, slamming the door screaming at the top of my lungs. *"Fuck!"*.

I headed back to my room to get my cellphone, so I could call my mom to give her the news we had to pay back rent or be evicted. When I made it back to the room, Dreka was sitting up in her bed, looking at me.

"Deja, what's wrong? I heard you yelling," Dreka stood to her feet stretching.

"Go wake your brothers up and go make y'all a bowl of cereal, please, and everything is okay. Don't worry," I lied, but she didn't need to worry about any of this shit my mother had going on.

I was looking through my phone, trying to figure out who I could call to help me out. I barely had any friends since I stopped hanging out some much. I remember a girl named Nikki, I met at the mall who told me they had auditions coming up for her job. I finally came across her number and texted her.

Me: *Hey, this is Deja from the mall, is your job still hiring?*

Nikki: *Hey, baes, and yes, we are, we're also looking to fire new girls. If you come down tonight, I can get you an audition with the boss man.*

Me: *Thanks, girl, I'll be there what's the address?*

Nikki: *2121 Market SW.*

AFTER I TEXT NIKKI, I TRIED CALLING MY MOM AGAIN. She still didn't answer. I threw my phone on the bed and walked out of my room, pissed off. I walked into the room. It was a mess, so I opened the blinds while the kids ate their breakfast and cleaned up the entire house. I was getting ready to take the trash out to the dumpster when my mother came walking up in the house, staggering smelling like piss and alcohol. Just the sight of her made me even angrier, I tried to hold my tongue, but I couldn't. I took the trash out and headed back towards our apartment. As I entered the apartment I walked in on my mom, who was whooping my three younger siblings. I quickly shielded them, snatching the belt out of her hands while pushing her back. I stood up, angry.

"What the fuck wrong with you, ma? Don't you ever in your life put your hands on them. They are just kids," I shouted with tears in my eyes. My siblings deserved better than this shit, she was putting them through.

I was ready to go to war with my mom, but I had other shit on my mind, and she wasn't one. I was trying to keep a roof over our heads.

"They are my kid's bitch you forgot I birthed your weird-ass too now show me some fucking respect," My mom slurred her word almost falling over.

I made the kids go to their rooms. My mom already exposed them to a lot of shit. I didn't want to worry about being homeless. I walk back to my room grabbing the notice taking it to my mom, when I handed it to her, she just stood there looking stupid.

"Yeah, if we don't come up with the thousand dollars by next week their evicting us. How could you be so fucking irresponsible? Running the streets more important than taking care of your kids and home, now I have to fix your fucking mistake before we are out on our ass," I yelled, getting emotional.

My mom rolled her eyes at the paper tossing it on the coffee table. Lying down before closing her eyes; it was still early, so I took the kids out while she slept her drunkenness off. When we made it back to the house, my mom was sitting on the front porch looking sober. I made the kids play so we could talk alone.

"I know Deja," my mother cut me off before I could say a word.

"Mom, this shit, you're doing not cool, and you were putting the kids at risk to be taken by the state with your reckless living. If something happened to you, I'd go crazy straighten up. I'm taking the kids before the state gets to them," I walked in the house heading to my room to get ready for my audition at the club.

———

A COUPLE OF HOURS LATER I WAS PULLING UP TO CLUB *X-rated*, I text Nikki letting her know I was there. I said a quick prayer before I walked into the club. It was live bitches dancing and stripping everywhere. I stood by the bar nervous, I turned to the bar to order a drink, but Nikki walked up on me. There was no backing out. I had to make some money fast. I followed Nikki to the boss's office, and my heart was in my mouth, I took a deep breath before walking in faking a smile. You could see the whole club scene from his office, especially the center it was beautiful all the LED lights gave the club a dope look.

Nikki introduced me. "This is Deja; I met her a few weeks ago at the mall. She looked for some work," Niki explained, offering me a seat on the futon in his office.

"Hello, Deja. You can call me X. Why, should I hire you," he extended his hand to me, shaking my hand. I pulled my hand back, sitting back, looking at him and Nikki.

I wiped my sweaty palms on my jeans speaking. "Look, I can't even lie to you right now; I need money fast so I can pay my rent so that I won't be out on my ass."

X lite a cigar before sitting back to listen to me talk about my problems, and why I was there. I was ready to do anything long as I got the job. As we sat there talking X office phone started ringing, he ignored it giving me his full undivided attention. X put his cigar out in the ashtray, stood up, walking over to me, cutting right to it.

"Can you dance?" He asked, sitting on his desk in front of me.

"Yes, I can" I admitted

"Good, I give all my girls nicknames. I'm going to call you *Elyte*; It means superior woman, your special believe it or not," X explained, reaching back to answer his ringing phone.

He almost snatched the phone out the wall when he answered it. I didn't say a word because he looked like the type not to play.

X yelled through the phone. "Send her ass up right now and send them other two bitches' home."

Nikki looked at me, telling me she was about to give me a tour of the club and show me where the locker room was. On the way out of X office, a light-skinned girl walked in pissed off talking crazy to X. I quickly followed Nikki.

ONAH

2013

Club XX-Rated

I was sitting in front of my locker when Star and Sky walked in. I couldn't stand their funky asses. They looked coked the fuck out of their minds. I looked up at Star and remembered that she owed me some money for doing a bachelorette party last weekend, but she never paid me.And since she was ducking and dodging my calls, I was going to approach her ass when we were in open space.

I yelled her name. "Star, can I holler at you real quick." I got up following her to her locker, cutting straight to it.

"What happened to you giving me my paper for doing that party with you and your sister? I have been calling and texting you. You ain't been answering me, so what the fuck going on?" I stood there looking at her waiting on her to talk, but she was too busy talking to the other bitches around us, and it pissed me off even more. I wasn't trying to fight tonight, but if it came down to it, I was.

"I thought Sky gave it to you," Star nonchalantly said as she walked off towards the makeup station.

I followed right behind her irritated, I felt my blood boiling, so I took a deep breath before talking to her.

"Star, I need my money, or I'm fucking you and Sky funny looking ass up, and that's on my momma," I gritted through my teeth, trying to be calm as possible.

Star smirked at me. "You not doing shit to me nor my sister bitch, you must have forgotten who put you on bitch. Since you want to make a scene, let's make one," Star barked, causing the other strippers to laugh.

I shook my head because I knew I was getting ready to cut up in the fucking locker room. I rolled my eyes walking off towards my locker, putting on my Nikes and Vaseline. I was tired of Star and Sky thinking muthafuckas feared them.

I walked back to the makeup station, and Star and Sky were standing there like they weren't about to get beat the fuck up. "Bitch, you got me fucked up," I yelled, punching the taste out of Star's mouth. She stood there looking at me. I was huffing and puffing I was going to dog walk her and her sister.

Star, Sky, and Nikki were X's top three money makers, and they thought they couldn't get touched. They felt they could run over me, but I wasn't having that shit anymore. Tonight X, and his bitches were going to get it. Star looked at me, holding her mouth crying. Her tears didn't move me. I turned to walk away when I felt someone jump on my back. When I looked in the mirror, it was Sky, Star's twin sister on me. I quickly backed into the mirror, shattering it. I saw Star coming full speed, so I tackled her dirty-looking ass. I threw blow after blow. They were going to know I wasn't the bitch to try and play with. I was going to get my shit one way or another. The other strippers stood around, looking. Security came running into the locker room. I felt my body being lifted off Star as I was beating her ass. Sky's ugly ass stood there watching me whoop her sister. I was glad I saw the fear in her eyes. After the fight was broke up, X wanted to see me in his office, and I was going to give him a piece of my mind too. When I walked into his office, I saw Nikki and some dark-skinned girls in X's office. The girl looked scared, but she wasn't my business to worry about.

"What the fuck you want, X? I need to go clean my locker out."

"Why are you cleaning out your locker Ocean?" X asked, excusing Nikki and the new girl from his office.

"Because I quit, I'm tired of you and your hoes trying to play me for stupid," I walked out of his office, ready to burn the whole club down with them in it.

When I made it to the locker room, Brinks and his men were cleaning up the broken mirror, and Star and Sky were nowhere to be found. I was cleaning out my locker when I saw Nikki walking the new girl through giving her the rundown, baby girl looked scared. I went to introduce myself to her so she could feel more comfortable.

"Hey, my name is Onah, but my stage name is

Ocean welcome to the X-rated don't let them suck you dry," I extended my hand shaking her hand, Nikki rolled her eyes and sucked her teeth, but I didn't give a fuck about her ugly ass anyways.

"Nikki, I got homegirl from here, go swallow the boss man dick like you always do," I sarcastically said to her. She looked at me rolling her eyes. I wanted to snatch her cheap-ass weave off her head and beat her ass too I felt they y'all were in cahoots.

"My name is Deja, but you can call me Elyte," Deja said as she sat down on the bench, looking scared.

I sat next to Deja so I could fill her in on who to fuck with and who not to.

"First thing first don't do business with Nikki, Star or Sky." As I was telling Deja, X's old ass walked into the locker room with Brinks on his heels, yelling my name.

"Ocean, can I talk to you real quick?" X mumbled, sticking his hands in his jacket.

I rolled my eyes then walked towards him. "What X? I don't have time for your bullshit".

I followed X to a dark room by the janitorial closet. I stood there looking at him, and he wasn't a bad-looking man, but his ways were fucked up.

"So, what's up X?" I stated licking my lips. I knew that shit drove him crazy when I did that.

"Whatever issue you got going on with Star and Sky that shit is dead and here is thirty-six hundred dollars they owed you plus a little extra for the inconvenience. You still have a job that's if you want it," X handed me the money then walked off.

I walked back into the locker room; I opened my locker, grabbed my bottle of Hennessey. I drank straight from the bottle. I went into my stash pulled out some coke I had left over from last night party. I made four lines then snorted two of them. I glanced over at Deja and offered her the mirror.

"Hit this. You'll be straight. We all were nervous our first-night dancing," Deja took the mirror from me. I nodded my head to let her know it was okay and to be easy.

I watched Deja snort the two lines like a pro. After her second line, she held her nose.

"It hurt oh my God," Deja said as her eyes started to water.

I took the mirror from Deja and ran my index finger over the mirror, getting the last little white specs that were left behind and put it in my mouth.

"Damn, girl take it easy," I took the mirror from her and handed her my bottle of Hennessey.

"You look familiar, Deja, you went to Central or something you look like this guy I know named Derrick are y'all related by chance?". I stepped back, getting a better look at her.

Deja dropped her head before answering. "Nah, I went to Union," Deja took her jacket off, put it in her locker. She then walked towards the showers with her Victoria Secret bag in her hand.

I couldn't figure out where I knew her from, I let it go for the time being, but I was determined to find out. Her face was very familiar to me, but it wasn't coming to me.

———

Two weeks later

I sat at the bar with Deja having a few drinks before our shift started, it had been two weeks since she started working at club X-Rated and we became very close. She had told me about her drama with her mother.

"I'm tired of living with my mom, she treats me like shit and those kids," Deja broke down crying. I thought it was the liquor, but I could tell she was hurt behind that. I wrapped my arm around her shoulder while she vented.

"Look, I have a spare bedroom with your name on it; if you want it, you can move in whenever you're ready, baby cakes," I told Deja as I got up from the bar.

"Can I move in tomorrow," Deja asked then followed me into the locker room.

Upon walking into the locker room, we ran into Star and Sky. I didn't speak to anyone of them anymore ever since they tried to play me. I told X I would keep the peace as long as they stayed in their lanes. Deja gave me a weird look as she headed towards the makeup station. Once I was completely ready to hit the floor, I noticed Deja was struggling to tie her shawl around her waist and boy did I get a rude awaken.

I bent down when I noticed how thick, Deja's sexy ass was. I was going to get her ass one of these days.

"You thick as fuck Deja," I joked, standing up straight, looking myself over in the mirror. I noticed Deja had a nervous grin on her face.

"Umm, thanks, I guess," Deja said shyly.

I licked my lips and looked her up and down. Deja must have sensed me trying to come onto her.

"I don't like girls, by the way," she blurted out. I smiled at her and walked out of the locker room, looking and feeling like a million bucks. I ended up on stage doing a solo dance since Nikki didn't show up, X asked me to fill in for her. The DJ played *Bando Jones* *"Sex You"* I twirled around the pole dancing. The stage was covered in money, and Deja stood there, hyping me up. I walked off the stage where all the niggas stood and laid on the floor, opened my legs, and twerked. Once my set was over, I collected my money, and Brinks walked me to the locker room so I could count my money. I looked around the locker room, but Deja wasn't in the locker room, so that meant she was still working the floor. After Deja made enough money, she was ready to leave for the night, and so was I. We cashed out and left, we then stopped by her mother's house to get her a change of clothes. When we arrived at her small apartment, her mom was still up drinking at four in the morning. Once she noticed Deja, she got off the couch following her upstairs. I stayed by the front door waiting on her. I heard Deja arguing with her mom.

"I need some more money, Deja, or the lights will get cut off," her mother yelled.

I was looking down at my phone when I looked up. I noticed Deja walked up the stairs. While upstairs, her mother went on and on about how bad of a daughter Deja was. It was the most awkward situation I had been in.

Deja looked at her mother, dead in the eyes. "Mom, I'm not giving you any more money; I just paid all the bills and rent, so try again," Deja snapped as she put her clothes in her overnight bag.

Deja's mom walked up to her and pushed her. "Fuck you, Deja, you not shit you, weird little bitch. You don't know what you like. Men or women just know what you are doing. God can see it," her mother barked.

My mouth almost hit the floor when her mom blurted that out. I knew I knew her from somewhere. I watched Deja turn toward her mother with tears in her eyes. I opened the front door and walked out when I looked back, Deja was behind me. We walked back to my car and got in. The whole drive to my house was quiet. I didn't know what to say. I parked my car we walked up to my front door, and I unlocked the door, I showed Deja the room she would be sleeping in, and she broke down crying.

"What's wrong Deja," I asked, grabbing a box of Kleenex out the hallway closet handing it to her.

She tried to talk in between the sobs, but I cut her off. "Get yourself together and meet me in the living room," I demanded before I walked to my room to change into something comfortable. Once I was changed, I went to the kitchen and grabbed two wine glasses and wine from my cellar. When I walked into the living room, I sat the stuff on the table and took a seat on my plush white sectional couch. Deja walked into the living room with bloodshot red eyes.

I patted the seat next to me. "Come sit and talk to me, tell me what's wrong."

"I'm bisexual, and I tried to hide it from my mother until she found out," Deja mumbled.

I poured wine into our glasses. "Yes."

"I like what I like, and I don't know why but I been trying to date men, but it hasn't been working. I've been trying to act like something I'm not, and it kills me," Deja confessed, taking a drink from her glass.

I sat there, shocked at the bomb that was just dropped on me. I had to drink out the bottle. I know a gay bitch when I see one.

"You have to swear to me you won't tell anyone," Deja pleaded with worried eyes.

I sat my glass on the table then grabbed Deja's hand. "I promise this our little secret."

"Since we're honest here, I might as well tell you this. I plan on opening my club one day. I'm tired of X and his girls thinking they run shit, I know I have what it takes," I mumbled.

I explained to Deja long as she was loyal to me shit was going to go by smooth with no problem. I had a plan, and I had to execute it soon, or it was going to be too late. We drunk the whole bottle of wine.

"Deja, do you see yourself messing with a girl like me?" I asked, popping open another bottle.

"I mean, I don't know. You're too masculine for me. I like my girl's girly in away.," Deja babbled.

"What if I told I like you?".

Deja raised her eyebrow, side-eyeing me asking. "Say what now?"

"You heard me," I got up, walked into the kitchen to put my glass in the sink. When I looked at the time, it was almost six-thirty in the morning. I walked straight to my bedroom falling out. Deja and I became best friends ever since that night we met at the club, but our bond grew over time. We became roommates and moved in together. We did everything together, and I mean everything. We worked hard to come up, and we did just that. A couple of months had gone by, and my plan was finally in motion. We were going to start our own empire.

Deja and I had started dating, and we eventually opened up our strip club on East Beltline called the *"Foxxy Kitten"*. After three years of stripping, we had everything, but the money was so good Deja, and I couldn't stop dancing.

I walked into our office, and Deja was on her phone, texting and smiling, and it somewhat pissed me off. I walked over to her catching her off guard.

"What you doing?" I asked and snatched her phone out her hand. I looked at the messages, and she was writing to a nigga named Tyrek.

Deja jumped up from the chair. "Give me my phone back now," she reached for her phone, but I pushed her out to the floor.

"So, you creeping with niggas now?" I shouted. My feeling was somewhat hurt.

Deja got up off the floor and dusted herself off. "Yeah, it's a nigga, Onah. We need one."

When Deja said that, I smacked the shit out of her. She snatched her phone from my hands and took off out of the office. I didn't run after her trifling ass. What can I say relationships can be rocky?

2
———

DEJA

I woke up late my alarm clock did not go off like it was supposed to, I did a private party that Onah had booked for me. I sat up in the bed looking at the time it was almost 4 P.M. I had a visit to see my kids at 3:30 P.M. I hurried up and called the caseworker, letting her know I was running late. I was making my life spiral out of control. I need to practice time management badly. While I was deep in my thoughts Onah walked in my room, snatching the curtains open. The sun was bright as hell.

"Damn, girl ain't you late for your visit with the kids," Onah pointed out to me, but I already knew I was late. I rolled my eyes at her.

I got out the bed, moving like a zombie, my body was hurting, and my head was spinning. I took a quick shower popped an aspirin and grabbed my iPhone of the charger to order a Lyft. I grabbed my hormone pills out of my purse noting my gun was in there. I made sure the safety was on and stuck it back in my purse. Being in the stripper game, it came with any risk, and I wasn't going to get caught slipping. I took my pills, downing it with a cold sprite. When I made it to the front door, my Lyft driver was pulling up right on time.

"Bye, Onah, I'll see you later tonight at the club," I yelled before walking out of the house, locking up the house. When I made it to the visitation, the caseworker was escorting the kids out of the room.

'Why are you taking them out the room, I'm here now," I asked with concerning eyes.

"Ms. Anderson, you are thirty-four minutes late. This is unacceptable. Showing up late," the caseworker whispered to me walking right passed me, and it took everything in me not to snatch her nappy head ass up. I took a deep breath before I got myself in more trouble.

"I know I'm late; I worked a double last night, and I overslept. Please let me see the kids for a few minutes, please," I begged with tears falling from my eyes.

The caseworker walked down the hallway until we reached an empty room. She let me spend twenty minutes with the kids before ending out visit. I looked at all three of my kids and told them they would be home shortly. The caseworker pulled me to the side to talk to me while the kids packed up their toys.

"Ms. Anderson, I can't do this again I can get in a lot of trouble by my boss and the State of Michigan for doing this for you, so please be on time next time," she walked back into the room getting the kids so they could go back to their foster family.

I saw my phone flash. I knew I had gotten a text message or a Facebook message. I ignored it. I didn't bother to see who it was until my phone started ringing.

"Hello," I snapped on whoever was on the other end of the line.

"Damn, hello to you too beautiful, are you are working tonight?" Brink's voice bombed through the phone.

Brinks was somewhat like Onah's and my security guard. He was a much older man looked to be in his late forties early fifties and stayed on my head about getting out the game before it was too late. He always made sure I was straight, but I knew he was looking out for me because I was Onah top money-making girl. I was Onah prize strippers at Foxxy's. I did all the private parties, and Brinks was the collector at every party. I looked at the time on my phone, and realized I was late for work, and I knew Onah was going to be on my ass.

"Hey, Brinks?" I said in a dry tone. I hated the life I was living, and I hated tricking even more.

While Brinks talked to me about Onah, I order another Lyft and walked down the street to the speedway on 44th and Kalamazoo. I swear he would not shut up, so I cut him off.

"I'll be there. Brinks keep Onah busy I'm in the lyft now on my way, and I don't want to be bothered with her," I hung the phone upon him before he could even reply. The six o'clock traffic was stupid. It took me fifteen minutes to get to work.

When I walked into the "Foxxy Kitten" I got sick to my stomach, I was tired of dancing, and I was ready for a new scene I wanted to own my own business or something. Upon walking, I ran into Onah. She looked pissed off, but I didn't care my kids came first. She was on my heels as I walked into the dressing room so I could change so I can hit the floor. She watched my every move, and that made me nervous as hell. Since I helped her buy the club, she has been acting as if she owned me.

"I don't mean to cut into you right now, Deja, but do you have that money from last night's party?" Onah demanded sitting down on the bench in front of my locker, blocking me from getting in.

"Shit, I don't know you tell me, boss lady," I scoffed.

I knew what happened to the money, but she didn't need to know what happened to it. For the last four months, she hasn't been paying me telling me she got it wrapped up investments and shit, but that didn't concern me. I needed my money so I could get the fuck on down and raise my siblings the proper way without the excess drama.

Onah rolled her eyes at me and walked off. I was finally able to get into my locker. I went to freshen up and put on my outfit so that I could hit the floor. I didn't have time for Onah shit at least, not tonight. When I hit the floor, the club was almost packed, nights like this Onah wanted me to work the shade room, and everything went down behind the black curtains. It was rare. I worked the floor, but tonight I was. I sat at the bar and ordered my favorite drink, *Sex on The Beach*.

I had drunk at least three *Sex on The Beaches*, and I was feeling it. I thought I was tripping when I felt someone touch my shoulder. I turned around to a handsome, tall, dark skin man with pretty white teeth

"Hey," I smiled at Tyrek. He had finally come up to the strip club to see me.

Tyrek smirked at me. "Can a nigga get a lap dance, sweetheart?"

"Yes, anything daddy paying for he can get," I said seductively, getting up from the bar staggering a little.

Tyrek found a booth way in the back. It was dark and just right. I didn't want Onah to see us and start hating. She knew I liked men too, so the day was coming.

I pushed Tyrek into the leather booth and climbed on top of his lap and started dancing

"So, what's took you so long to come to see me," I asked in a seductive tone.

"I don't know I thought you were a catfish for real," he stated then smacked my ass, and it hurt like hell, but I played it off.

"Sure, tell me anything," I whispered in his ear, nibbling on his earlobe.

When I looked up in the mirror, Onah was standing there looking at the both of us. She interrupted what we had going on.

"Deja, I need you to work the shade room Rhonda called out, and I need an extra girl," when Onah said that I got pissed off instantly, I felt her cockblocking.

"I'm not working the shade room tonight I'm busy." I gave Tyrek all my undivided attention and Onah got jealousy and snatched me off of him,

"Bitch get off and go do what I said," Onah barked.

I got up from Tyrek's lap and fixed my outfit, and he grabbed my hand. Onah stood there looking pissed off, but I didn't care I was going to see Tyrel whether she likes it or not.

"I have to go, Ty. I'll see you around," I snatched my hand away from him, walking off toward the shade room irritated with Onah ass. She was going to hear my mouth whenever I ran into her again.

3
____

ONAH

I was sitting in my office, counting the money I made the night before, but shit was not adding up. I recounted it three times, and I was still coming up short. I called my security guard Brinks in my office so he could make a bank run and deposit the money before the bank closed.

"When you make the deposit the money into the account make sure you call me do you understand me," I barked at him

Once he left, I locked my office door and went to the bar to have a drink. I needed to sit where I could see Deja ass when she came walking through the door. I had my bartender Sexxy Lexxy make me a drink. Shit was starting to get crazy between me, and Deja and Lexxy was the only female I could talk to besides Deja. We were starting to go our separate ways. I wanted to get more money, and she wanted to get out of the game, but it was just getting started.

When Deja walked into the club, all eyes were on her. She looked irritated and sleepy. I needed to talk to her about what happened last night. She walked right passed me as if she didn't see me sitting there.

"Lexxy, make sure you put these in Deja drink if she orders anything to drink tonight," I passed her three white pills sliding them across the counter before walking away following Deja to the locker room. The bouncer I had watching the door opened the door for Deja and me.

"Hey, boss lady, what are you doing back here?" Brinks asked, closing the door.

"Personal call," I mumbled, walking into the dark locker room, tucking my gun under my shirt. When I walked in strippers were sitting around talking and drinking as if there wasn't money out there to be made.

"What the fuck y'all doing sitting around this bitch like ain't money out there. Hit the muthafuckin floor now," I barked at all my girls while looking at Deja ass.

I couldn't look at Deja anymore. I walked off, heading out the club. I had a business meeting to attended to at the *Holiday Inn Express*, and I couldn't keep him waiting. I jumped in my car, hitting the highway doing 95 mph on 131 south. When I made it to the hotel, Ty was standing outside by the sliding doors smoking a blunt. That's one thing I liked about him; he didn't give a fuck about what people thought of him. I parked my truck and got out, pulling my pencil skirt down, meeting him halfway across the parking lot. His cologne smelled so good, I smelled him before he even touched me, and that made me weak in the knees.

"What's good boo," Ty hugged me tight as hell, almost breaking my damn back.

"Let me the fuck go. How could you talk to Deja after what we been through?" I asked, pissed off.

Tyrek chuckled. "Man, Onah, don't start this bull shit. If you just be honest with your girl, this would go over smoothly, but nah, you have to be difficult," Tyrek spat.

I got a good look at his fine ass. He handed me the room key.

"We on the fifth floor in suite five hundred fifteen," he said, and I took the key and headed towards the elevators.

I went up to the room and fell in love the moment I walked in the room. Ty had gone shopping for me, there were shopping bags everywhere but what caught my eye was the jewelry box sitting on the marble table by the bed. When I opened it, my mouth almost hit the floor. It was a diamond necklace. I couldn't take my eyes off of it. I walked to the mirror, seeing how it looked on my neck. I was so stunned by the necklace that I didn't hear Ty walk into the room.

"Thank you, you know you didn't have to do this Ty

I get money I can spoil myself but thank you," I walked to the mini-refrigerator taking a bottle of wine out of it.

I sat on the bed, popping the bottle open. I drank straight from the bottle I was stressed out. Ty was chopping up a few lines while snorting and talking on his phone like I wasn't in the bathroom taking a bubble bath. The conversation must have gotten heated because I heard him throw his phone, and it broke. I walked out the shower with a white plush towel around my body, Ty stared at me as if I was a steak or something. I sat next to him on the couch, feeling tipsy. He started kissing on me. It's like I fell under his spell. Ty had done somethings to my body I had never experienced, he put coke on my pussy and snored it off licking the residue off. I felt terrible fucking other niggas on Deja when she was loyal, but our relationship was starting to fade. She didn't have a dick, and Ty did, and from time to time, I needed to feel the real thing. So for the night, I was going to live and fuck Ty all night. Ty fucked me all night long until the sun came creeping through the curtains I was exhausted I couldn't lift my head off the pillow when I looked at the time. I laid back down until I heard Ty wrestling putting on his clothes, I rolled over to him fully dressed.

"Where are you going, Ty, I thought we were kicking it," I wrapped the white sheet around my body, jumping to my feet fast hell.

"I'll be back ma, I have to go meet up with my homie about my money from a job we did last week," Ty grabbed his jacket, leaving me in the room looking dumb. I took a quick shower and put on my clothes heading home before Deja got there.

4
<hr>

DEJA

After I danced on stage, I did a few tables dances last night, and I went home early, I wasn't feeling it. I cashed out paying my pay cut to Brinks so he could give it to Onah since her ass went MIA out of nowhere last night ain't nobody seen her ass. I text Tyrek to let him know I could only meet during the daytime because I was busy at night. When he called and asked me to go to breakfast with him, I was down, plus a bitch was hungry too. I had to go to court later that morning, so breakfast was a good start for me. I pinned my curls up, walking into the shower. The water felt good hitting my body, but it also woke me up. Once I stepped out, I dried off, putting on my court clothes. I put on an olive-green little top that I order from Fashion Nova with a pair of blue jeans with a pair of open-toe gold heels. Once I was completely dressed, I did my makeup and walked out the door. I took an

Uber to Ann's house for breakfast. It where I met Tyrek. He was looking like everything to me. He was the perfect gentleman to me. We ate and talked, once we were done Tyrek offered to give me a ride to the courthouse.

"If you don't mind me ask ma', why don't you have a car and your stripping?" Ty found a parking spot on the next street over from the courthouse.

"To be honest I could have a car note, but I have other shit I have to handle right now that's not a priority for me right now," I admitted getting out of the car as I was getting ready to cross the street Tyrek caught up to me, I looked at him as if he was crazy.

"If you don't mind, sweetheart, I would like to be your support for the day. I canceled all my meetings for this morning, so I'm all yours until noon," Ty blurted out putting money in the meter.

Walking into court, I felt like I was going to have a panic attack my heart was racing, and my head felt like it was going to explode. I said a quick prayer under my breath. My lawyer was waving at me, and I knew she wanted to talk to me. I told Ty to have a seat; it was going to be a while.

"I'll be back, Ty. I have to handle something," I walked off, hoping for good news.

I had tears in my eyes when my lawyer told me my siblings might be coming home sooner than we had thought. I completed all my parenting classes, and I got my GED, so I was going to attend Community College while my kids were in school during the day. After we spoke in the hallway, we walked back into the courtroom, and the judge called my name. My heart dropped. I was ready to be done dealing with the state. I had just bought and paid my house off, I had fifteen grand saved in the bank, so I was more than ready. When the judge approved the kid's overnight visits, I was ready to jump out of my skin. I was crying real tears of joy. I was one step closer to my goals of bringing them home where they belonged. After court let out, Ty dropped me off at home, asking if he could see me some other time.

"Let me take you out sometimes, Deja," Ty walked me to the front steps waiting on me to answer him.

I smiled, turning around to walk up the stairs. "I'll text you and thank you for taking me to court today" I walked into the house after Ty pulled off. I closed the door kicking off my heels, grabbing my laptop from under the couch. I went online ordering everything I needed for my house and the kids. I was so deep into picking bedroom sets out that I didn't hear the keys or Onah walk in. I looked up at her; she looked pissed off.

"Girl, why are you walking up in here looking like you mad at the world?" I sat my laptop down and got her a bottle of water out the refrigerator.

"I am mad, my business meeting didn't go as planned last night, so I booked me a five-star hotel and took myself shopping to feel better, but it didn't help," Onah confessed.

Onah sat her shopping bags on the floor. Taking off her heels, she set her purse on the coffee table and laid down with her face buried in the pillow. I felt terrible for her; she was starting to look old as hell, and we were only twenty-five years old. I tried to comfort her, but she told me to get the fuck away from her.

"I know you not in the mood to talk Onah, but I need to throw a party. I'm moving out at the end of this month, and I want to make sure I have my bills paid up so I won't have to worry about shit when the kids come home," I let the truth slip through my lips not realizing what I was saying until Onah sat up staring daggers into me.

"You want me to set up another party, but you don't know where the fuck my money at from the last party Deja," Onah yelled, turning red in the face.

"I told you I didn't get paid so holler at the nigga you booked the party with or Brinks," I walked into my room, slamming the door knocking a picture of Onah and me off my wall. It was of us at the grand open of the club. We were so happy at one point, but shit was all bad. Now that the state was allowing me to get my sibling's, I noticed Onah been acting funny.

I picked the picture up, feeling sad. I just wanted to go back to being the cool happy friends we were a few years ago. The happiness we once had was starting to fade away, we stayed arguing about the dumbest shit and fighting.

AFTER ONAH PULLED THAT LITTLE STUNT THE OTHER night, I haven't been back to the club or did any private parties. I had finalized the deal on my house, I couldn't stay under her roof another month, or I was going to end up on snapped. I found a lovely five-bedroom home with two bathrooms in the Burton Heights area. I was so close to getting my siblings out of the system, my mother lost custody of them two years ago, and I been trying my hardest to get them back. The State of Michigan was on my ass. I had to take parenting classes and random drug tests. They were getting ready to start their overnight visits, and Onah house was not fit for children; she was always doing some wild as shit. I met up with the realtor and signed the paperwork process after that. I headed back home. When I walked into the house, Onah was sitting in the living room on the couch watching Roxanne on Netflix. I walked right passed her, going into the kitchen.

"Damn, Hi, to you too, bitch," Onah yelled in my direction. I still ignored her ass.

Hearing Onah's voice aggravated me to the point I was ready to snap her fucking neck. I put some grapes in a bowel and rinsed them off before I sat on the front porch soaking up some sun. Onah walked onto the porch sparking small conservation I wasn't inter-ested in. The sundress I had on was long when I kicked my legs up on the railing. It came up my thighs. I caught Onah, staring hard as hell at my thighs. Onah sat in front of me and put her hand up my dress and played with my freshly Brazilian waxed pussy. I hated she knew exactly how to touch and please me, and she put me back under her spell. I began to moan, and I felt myself getting ready to cum, and she stopped finger me. I could have cried how bad the feeling of cuming was stuck. I cried out, begging her to finish.

"Please don't stop, Onah." I sobbed, begging her to finish. Onah got up and walked in the house I followed right behind her. She sat on the couch, and I stood in front of her removing my sundress, exposing my pierced nipples and pussy. I crawled on top of her laying her on the couch tongue kissing her. I removed her bra and panties. I slipped a finger in her, and she was wet as hell. Onah smacked my ass, and that turned me on even more.

"Turn that ass around and put that pussy on my face," Onah demanded. I flipped my body putting my pussy in her face and putting my head between her legs we were getting ready to sixty-nine each other. I couldn't focus Onah was sucking my soul out my body. I tried to get away, but she wrapped her arms around my legs. She nibbled and licked on my pussy, causing me to cut back to back. I was in pure ecstasy. My body trembled, and I couldn't stop shacking Onah smacked my ass. Again, causing me to moan out her name.

"Go lay in the bed. I'll be there in a minute," Onah beamed with excitement.

My pussy was leaking with every step I took, I laid in the bed, and Onah appeared in the room with a strap on. We had never used dildos before, so it was new to me. I sat up in the bed, horny as hell. I stuck two fingers in my pussy so she could see how wet I was. She crawled onto the bed and spread it my legs she thrust in and out of me until I squirted all on the sheets begging her to stop I had enough. Once Onah fucked me in every position possible, she removed the strap on, and we started scissoring each other cuming instantly. I went on to take a shower, but I couldn't move. We laid there in those wet sheets until we drifted off into a deep slumber. I woke up to Onah, going through my cell phone. I jumped up, snatching my phone out her hand.

"What the fuck Onah," I got out the bed, furious ready to fight her ass.

"So, you really doing this to me? What, I don't take good care of you or something," Onah snapped back-handing me.

I was fighting the tears back; my face was stinging. I hated Onah didn't respect me as a person, and that was the last straw her putting her hands on me.

"I have to move to get my siblings out the system you know my situation. Nah don't act like that," I walked out her room headed to my bedroom I had enough of her for the day.

"Them not your fucking kids, fuck them little bastard. Their better off with the state anyways," Onah shouted at the top of her lungs. I stopped dead in my tracks and turned around, ready to spit in Onah fucking face.

"They are my kids; I may not have had them personally, but they are my siblings, and long as I'm breathing, they won't be in foster care bitch. Your just mad I'm leveling up and bought a house, I don't need shit from you," I walked off leaving Onah dumb ass standing right there in the hallway.

5

ONAH

The shit Deja said to me fucked me up a little bit. Maybe I was afraid of her leaving me. I don't know what happened to us. Money was the root of all evil and causing us to hurt each other. The first time I ever fucked with a girl, it was Deja, and I fell in love with the bitch. After our argument, I went to my room and called up Ty to see why he ghosted me. I sat on my bed and lit my blunt. I needed to ease my mind before calling Tyrek ass. I hit my blunt a couple of times, coughing my damn lungs up. I put my blunt out and grabbed my cellphone from the nightstand and dialed up Ty's number. To my surprise, he answered on the first ring.

"What happened to you this morning Ty? You played me like I was a baldheaded ass stepchild," I snapped on him. I was ready to hang the phone up because I knew he was about to say some dumb ass shit.

Niggas wonder why I don't fuck with them like that. Ty is the prime example of why I never wasted my time. I loved fucking with bitches better; they fucking listened when I said something. I laid across my bed listening to him tell me a dumb as story about being caught up.

"Let me take you dinner tomorrow night, Onah," Ty voice always did something to me. I was mad at him, but my body was reacting differently.

"How, about I make you dinner, you come over, and we'll go from there. How does that sound?" I got up from my bed, looking out the window seeing Deja sitting on the front porch with her head down. I swallowed my pride and went to check on her I have been a bitch lately, and I was wrong for saying the shit I did earlier.

When I walked outside, Deja was texting on her phone. She had a smile on her face as if she was enjoying the conversation. I sat beside her, not saying a word, I missed moments like this where we could read each other mind and just vent, but now I couldn't tell what was going on with her.

"Look, Dej, you know I hate apologizing and shit, but I was wrong for what I said earlier about your siblings I had no right," I sniffed, wiping my tears away.

I looked at Deja, and I couldn't read her facial expressions at all, I was getting mixed emotions from her ass. I was getting ready to say fuck her until she looked up at me and told me what she been going through.

"Onah, shit hasn't been the same with us in years as best friends or lovers. You try to control everything I do. I'm tired of that this shit we are doing right here. I'm physically and mentally drained. I risked everything to keep you happy now it's time I do what makes me happy and that's me getting my siblings and making their lives better," Deja dropped a whole load on me sitting on the porch, and for the first time I felt where she was coming from. Deja did everything in her power to make me happy from the time we were twenty years old until now. I got up, went into the house, and made a few phone calls. When I walked on the porch, Deja was gone, so I sent her a text message letting her know what was up.

Me: *You got your wish, one last party this Saturday at the Baymont Inn*

Deja: *Cool, thank you, Onah. Thanks for being so understating babe XOXO*

Me: *No problem, what are best friends for.*

I got myself together so I could head to my club. I know Brinks was worried about me. I sent him a text message letting him know to have all the girls lined up outside my office so I could see who was sent to the party Saturday night with Deja. If Deja and the girls follow through at the party, I was going to make 250,00. A local rapper from Chicago requested my top girls, and he was going to get what he asked for. I was that bitch. I couldn't be touched. I had GRPD on payroll, so I never had to worry about my shit coming crashing down.

"Hey boss lady," Sexxy Lexxy shouted over the music. She had on a lime green see-through tank top on. You could see that her nipples were pierced and that shit was a turn on, especially on a chocolate bitch with pretty nipples.

"What's up, Lexxy, you looking good boo," I flirted with her pretty ass walking to my office.

When I made it to my office, the girls were lined up outside my office, looking like they were getting to audition for a movie or something. They all spoke at once, sounding like a robot, "Hello, Onah."

I opened the door to my office, and Brinks was sitting there counting money. I hired Brinks because he was a big nigga, and I knew niggas weren't going to try him, plus he was dead as fuck. X knew what he was doing when he hired Brinks. When he found out I was opening my club, I brought him aboard. I sat my purse on my desk taking a sit, I noticed I had an email, but I ignored them for the moment. I chopped it up with Brinks before checking out my girls for the party for Saturday night. It was a knock at the door, and Sexxy Lexxy stepped it made me lose my train of thought that's how fine she was.

"Come in and close the door, baby girl," I closed my laptop, giving her all of my attention.

"I wanted to talk to you about something if you have the time," Lexxy paused at the door, looking scared.

"Your good, what's up?" I got up from my desk to pour myself a well deserved stiffed drink.

"I was wondering if I could do the private party this Saturday, I need to catch up on my bills," Lexxy sat back in the chair looking at me waiting on an answer.

I sat back down at my desk, debating how I was going to answer. I didn't take her as a dancer even though she had a banging ass body.

"Let me think about it. I'll let you know Friday night," I explained to her opening my laptop back up. Lexxy seemed pissed off, but I didn't care. I felt like she wasn't cut out to do what my girls did. The shade room prepared them for parties like the ones I booked. I just wanted my night to go by smoothly as possible. I turned the light off in my office, laying my head on my desk. I was tired if I was going to make it through the night, I needed to take a nap. Before dozing off the clock read 7 pm when I woke up with was almost midnight. Brinks was banging on my damn office like the police. When I opened the door, the police had a warrant in my face. They pushed me out the way and tore my office up.

"What the fuck is this," I yelled at the officer with the warrant in his hand. Being pissed off was an understatement.

I tried calling Deja, but she was not answering me

that pissed me off even more. I decided to go downstairs and check on my girls, but I was stopped and put in handcuffs. This was bad for business and social media. My girls that worked the shade room got booked also, they shut my shit down. As I was being put in the back of the police car, Deja appeared looking worried.

"Bail me out by tonight," I was embarrassed my face was plastered all over the news, and that was bad for me and my business. I sat in that cold jail for over twelve hours before Deja ass bonded me out of jail. I was lucky I got charged on racketeering, but I knew I was going to beat that petty ass shit. When I walked out of the Kent county jailhouse, Deja was standing there looking tired and irritated.

"What took you so fucking long to bail me out Dej," I walked up to her, almost smacking the fucking taste out her mouth.

"You didn't have any money. I had to use my money to bail your ungrateful ass out," Deja yelled, stepping back, making sure I didn't hit her.

"What the fuck you're talking about, I have plenty of money put up," I barked at her snatching my car keys out her hands heading to my truck. Deja was right on my heels.

"What I'm saying somebody is stealing from you because you had no money in your safe when I tried to go take money out of it.

I dropped my head trying to gain composure of my

anger, I never listen to Deja, and she warned me because she never got paid from the last party and Brinks was supposed to make sure she got that money. Now shit was starting to add up. I hit the steering wheel until my hands started hurting. I looked at myself in the mirror, and I looked like shit; my hair was all over the place, and my face had a scratch on it from the pigs being too rough. I finally found the courage to start my truck and pull out of the county jail parking lot. The whole drive home was quiet, I was pissed off, and somebody was going to pay for the shit that was going on. When I turned my cellphone on, I had so many missed calls and voicemails. I saw that Ty called and texted me, but I didn't bother to read it. I was focused on finding Brinks bitch ass.

"Thank you, Deja, for bonding me out," I tried to hug her, and she jumped, and that made me feel like more shit. I dropped Deja off at home and headed to my club when I got there Brinks car was not there. I parked my car and unlocked my doors to my club. They fucked my club up, tables and chairs were knocked over. I walked into the shade room, instantly getting pissed off. They cut the leather in my private booths.

"FFUUCCKKKKKK!!!!!!!," I snapped, picked a bottle up, and tossed it at the mirror, shattering it.

6

DEJA

I had finally moved in my house, the shit after Onah being charged with racketeering I cut all ties with her months ago, she had too much going on, and I was ninety days away from bringing my kids home for good. Tyrek helped me move; he even helps set the kid's room up. We had gotten close over the last couple of months. I wasn't ready for a relationship or to have sex, and he respected that. In the middle of unpacking my living room, Onah rang the doorbell. I wasn't expecting any company, so it through me off to why she was even at my front. I opened the door, ready to cuss her ass out, but quickly stopped myself when I noticed how she was looking.

"What the fuck happened to you, Onah?" She was looking bad. Her hair was messed up, and her clothes were dirty, and she smelled.

"They got everything I worked so hard for. They

took everything from me," Onah broke down crying I had never seen her like that, so I knew it was serious. I allowed her to come to my house. She was looking awful. I excuse myself going upstairs to get her a warm soapy cloth so she could clean her face. My cellphone started ringing, so I had Tyrek take her the washcloth while I received a collect call from my mother.

"Hey mom, what's up I'm in the middle of something right now can you call back later or tomorrow," I didn't give her enough time to answer I hung up and went back downstairs.

Tyrek and I sat talking while Onah ate her ham and cheese sandwich. The way Onah was staring at him made me feel some type of way. It was getting late, and I was ready to soak in my brand-new tub.

"Onah, I'm getting ready to call it a night, you can come back tomorrow after I get out of class," I stood up walking towards the door when I heard Onah crying I turned around, and her face was beet red.

"I don't have anywhere to go Dej, can I please just stay the night, I promise to be gone before you wake up," Onah pleaded her case, and I felt terrible.

I looked up at Tyrek, and he gave me a look telling me to be nice.

"You can just for tonight," I pointed out, showing her where she would be staying. After I got Onah to settle in, I went to my room and ran a nice hot lavender bubble bath. I relaxed, loving the peace. I watched Ty lay across my bed and watch *ESPN* sport highlight.

When I got them out the tub, Ty was sleep, so I snuggled right up to him and fell asleep. I woke up to the smell of bacon and eggs in the air I got out of bed grabbing my housecoat heading downstairs. I made it to the kitchen Tyrek was cooking up a storm listening to *Biggie Smalls*.

"Boy, what the hell you in here doing ruining my new kitchen," I joked with him sitting at the island in the middle of the kitchen.

I noticed the room Onah slept in bedroom door was still closed, I got up from my chair, making my way towards the room when Ty stopped me halfway. He had a weird look on his face, and I couldn't figure out just yet what was wrong with him.

"Why is the door still closed she is supposed to be gone, Ty," I raised my voice, sitting back in my chair.

"Chill Dej, Onah needs you right now. I know she was a shitty friend to you, but you need to do the right thing," Ty kissed me on the forehead, walking out the kitchen leaving me there to think about what he had just said.

The shit Onah put me through was fucked up, ever since she found out my secret, I felt like she was always trying to use that against me. I was still making sure she was straight, putting her before me. She treated me like a fucking rag, and I was tired of being stepped on and used by her. Only if Ty knew about our relationship. I ate my food in silence, thinking of a master plan to get Onah for the fuck away from me and fast. I cleaned up my mess and put the dish in the dish-washer. I went back to my room to get dressed so I could dress for my morning classes at Grand Rapids community college. Ty watched me get dressed while lying in bed. I grabbed his car keys and headed out the door once I kissed him on the lips.

7

____

ONAH

When Tyrek came downstairs last night, I thought I was dreaming, I was at my lowest, and he disappeared on me when I needed him the most. To find out he been fucking with Deja killed me a little bit. I knew him first, and I thought we had a bond, but I guess the fuck not. I had lost everything the bank froze all of my funds I was out on the streets homeless. Ms. Bad ass Onah broke who would have thought. It was cold out I didn't have any more money I had to swallow my pride and find Deja. I expected Deja to turn her back on me, but to my surprise, she had her welcomed me with open arms. To see Tyrek come from Deja's stairs that hurt my feelings, but I played it off smooth so that Deja wouldn't find out. I was glad when she showed me the room. I was going to be sleeping in for the night I haven't slept in a comfortable bed since I lost my apartment. After Deja showed me my room and gave me a fresh towel set, I went into the bathroom across the hall from me. I walked into the bathroom and turned on the light, and quickly cut the shower on. While the water was heating up, I looked at myself in the mirror, and I looked a hot ass mess. My hair was all over the place, and my nose was red as hell. I checked the temperature on the water. Once it was hot enough, I quickly got undressed and got in the shower. I cried in the house being this low really fucked me up. I washed my hair than my face and scrubbed the rest of my body. Once I felt clean enough. I rinsed off, then got out and dried off. I wrapped the towel around my body and went back to the room. I sat on the bed and applied some lotion to my body that Deja had in the room. Once I got done, I laid across the bed, thinking about my life when I dozed off. When I woke up the next morning early as hell. I got up and got dressed. Once I was dressed, I walked the room, and I ran into Ty, and he stopped me from leaving.

"Where you going, Onah?" Ty turned on the living room light sitting on the couch as I cracked the front door.

"Deja told me to leave her house by daylight, and I'm respecting her wishes," I opened the door. Ty got up from the couch, closed the door, then backed me into the corner hovering over me.

"You, not going anymore, Onah, go take that shit off and wash it, you stink! This is not the same bad bitch that I met a year ago. You gave up on yourself?" Ty pushed my hair out my face to get a better look at me. I was starting to feel like I was doing something wrong, but Deja stole him from me first. *"My fuck this bitch attitude."* was beginning to surface, and I had to push her back in. I walked away from Tyrek and went into the kitchen so I could go to the mudroom where the washer and dryer were. I took my clothes off, and Ty reappeared with a *PINK* outfit with the tag still on it. I took it from him and put it on.

"So, do Deja know about us?" I asked, as I zipped my jacket up, looking Ty, dead in the eyes.

"No, and it's going to stay like that. She won't have to know if you keep your mouth shut. We were never that serious, so she doesn't need to know about my past," Ty looked over his shoulder to make sure no one was there. After I started the washer, I went back to the room Deja had me, and I laid back down, and Ty laid his ass down with me every bone in my body told me to get the fuck up, but I couldn't. Ty had a way with the ladies. He was very comforting. When Ty kissed me, I felt weak and gave in. He made love to every inch of my body. I laid there in bliss. I knew at any given moment Deja was going to wake up and catch us. I end up falling back to sleep until I heard Deja and Ty voice in the kitchen. I so badly wanted to eat my stomach was growling and hurting I didn't want to run into Deja, so I stayed in the room until I heard her leave out the garage door. I finally got up, I changed the sheet, and I cleaned up my mess, I had a plan to get my shit back and take back what belongs to me.

8

DEJA

Onah thought she was slick coming back into my life, but it wasn't going to be that easy for her. I couldn't concentrate sitting in my psychology class; the new hormone pills I was taking were making me feel blah and tired all the time. It was almost time for my yearly checkup, and I had questions about the new medication. Once my lecture was over, I headed home. I hated the wintertime; it was always a hassle to drive thank God Tyrek had heated seats in his car. When I walked in the house, it smelled good, the smell of greens and neckbones was the first thing I smelled. Onah was in my kitchen cooking and dancing around in my kitchen.

"Umm, what do you think you're doing, Onah?" I asked her, sitting my bag on the countertop, walked into the kitchen.

"Cooking dinner." She yelled.

I needed to lay down. I felt like I had to throw up, and the room was spinning. I heard Onah call my name but ignored her. I grabbed the remote, turned on *Netflix*. Onah brought me a cup of tea with honey she sat down on the side of me she looked worried.

I looked up at her breaking the silence between us. "Can you please get me a bucket I'm about to puck." My mouth got water, and I had started throwing up all on my throw rug and table.

Onah took off, running towards the kitchen. I tried to lay back down, but I couldn't stop throwing up. Onah handed me a black bucket, once I finally stopped throwing-up I headed upstairs I needed a hot shower. I didn't like the way Onah was looking at me.

"Why, you staring at me like that?" I raised an eyebrow at her side-eyeing her.

"I'm worried about you Dej, I know shit ain't right between us, but I'm worried about you," Onah explained.

I made my way to my master bathroom with Onah on my heels. I sat the bucket down by the toilet and looked at Onah. "It's my anxiety. It's like the closer the date comes for these kids to come home, I freak out," I stated, sitting on the edge of the tub.

Onah wrapped her arm around me. "You got this, Deja. Don't second guess yourself."

I turned the shower. I had started to think about how my life was really getting ready to change. When Onah left the bathroom, I took my shower. After I got out of the shower, I laid in the bed with a cold rag over my eye's it was still early in the evening. I drifted off to sleep, forgetting that Onah was even there. I woke up to my bedroom, pitch black. I looked at the clock. It was almost eleven-thirty at night, and Ty was not in bed. I went downstairs to look for him, and he still wasn't home. Onah was sitting in the living room reading a book, by one of my favorite authors, *"When a Gangsta Falls in Love" by Robin.*

She spoke to me without taking her eyes off the book, smiling. I wasn't in the mood for any funny shit. "What the fuck so funny?" I rolled my eyes at Onah.

"Damn, girl, stop tripping. I was smiling because this book is crazy good," Onah snapped on me. I sat the book down on the table.

I walked into the kitchen, trying to make myself a plate of food, but the food was gone. Onah grabbed a plate of food out the microwave handed it to me. I gave her the side-eye. I fully didn't trust her, so her being nice was suspect as fuck. I sat at the dining-room table eating when Ty walked into the house. I rolled my eyes at him. He tried to kiss me, but I declined him. He smelled like weed and liquor. I finished eating my food, glaring at his ass.

Ty broke the silence speaking to me. "Bae, why are you looking at me like that?". Ty took off his jewelry at the table.

"Where you been at? It's almost midnight, you ain't called or text me all day," I stood up, and walked into the kitchen. I ran into Onah, eating a bowl of ice cream. She had that bitch you know what he been doing look on her face. I dismissed her facial expression and put my plate in the dishwasher. I walked right passed Tyrek headed to my room. I laid across the bed, scrolling Instagram when I noticed two girls standing in front of Onah club, basically saying they were the new club owners. I dug deeper into it. I started following the page when I noticed who they were. I jumped up, ran downstairs to see Onah.

"Onah! You need to come to see this bitch," I yelled, as I walked into the kitchen, she and Ty were having a conversation. It bothered me because they stopped talking the moment I walked into the kitchen, and that didn't sit with me well at all.

Onah looked at me. "Look, it's Star and Sky?" I told her and handed her my phone so that she can see.

Onah's mouth hit the floor after spending five minutes scanning the picture.

"Wait, so everything that happened to me was because of them so they could take my club from right underneath my nose," Onah hit the countertop pissed off.

Tyrek stood there, looking at me, trying to figure out what was going on. Onah went to get her phone and came back into the kitchen. She was going the fuck in. I didn't want to be whoever that was on the other end. She hung the phone, slamming it on the kitchen table. She was red in the face, and I could tell she was fighting the tears.

"What the fuck was that about Onah?" I questioned her.

Onah put her head down. She looked defeated.

"It's Star and Sky," Onah yelled sobbing. The shit she was saying wasn't making any sense until she broke it down to me.

Onah looked at me, crying. I mean boohoo with snot coming from her nose. For the first time in a long, I felt terrible for her. I handed her a napkin and hugged her because she needed it. Tyrek sat there looking at us with a confused look on his face, so I filled him in on what happened five years ago.

I looked at him, taking a deep breath. "When I first started working at Club X-Rated Onah was telling me it was her last night dancing and to be careful not to trust a lot of the girls there. Long story short, Onah and I did our thang saving up enough money to buy her club," I stopped and looked down at Onah.

" I helped her build her brand. She would book parties for the girls and me until the whole operation came crashing down on her a couple of months back. When it happened, I kept telling her shit wasn't adding up now. It all makes sense," I stated, looked at Onah as she dried her eyes.

Tyrek didn't say a word. After I dropped that bomb on him, he looked at Onah and me and asked us the million-dollar question.

"So, what y'all gonna do about them, bitches?". Ty walked out of the kitchen, leaving Onah and me to come up with a plan.

I turned to Onah, told her what I was going to do. "Look, Onah, I'll help you, but after this, I'm done dealing with you. I will set a meeting up with the twins to get to the bottom of this bullshit," I walked out the kitchen and headed back to my room so I could get some sleep.

Upon walking into my room, Ty was ass naked, stroking his dick in the middle of the bed. I closed the door stood there looking at him jack off. I took off my clothes, exposing my hard nipples, I was beyond horny and way overdue for some dick. I crawled onto the bed. I grabbed his dick staring at his pretty dick. I took him into my mouth and went to work. I sucked until I couldn't suck anymore. Ty smacked me on the ass.

"Lay down and open your legs," Tyrek demanded. I did what he said. He started kissing my inner thighs, and that shit drove me crazy. I laid there, enjoying everything he did to me. Ty tried to slide up in me raw. I sat up was quick as hell.

"I know we been together for almost six months, but you're not fucking me unprotected. It's not happing. I don't need a slip up fucking our relation-ships up," I told him then got up from the bed and went into my nightstand draw and pulled a condom out.

"Deja, you need to calm down ma, I'm not a trifling

as nigga I know my dick clean. I haven't fucked anyone since I saw you, I swear to God," Ty pleaded.

He took the condom out my hand. He got up from the bed and went into the bathroom, and I followed him. Tyrek turned on the shower.

"Get in with me," Tyrek smiled at me, and I gave in. I replied. "Yes."

I walked into the shower, and Tyrek walked into the shower shortly after me. He picked up a sponge and rubbed it on my back, and it felt good, I turned to face him. We stood there, letting the hot water hit our body. Ty kissed me passionately, and I kissed him back, he picked me up penetrating me, I whined because it hurt until after a few strokes. With every stroke, he gave me, I fell deeper in love. He put me down, bending me over the bench in the shower, sliding back in going to work. My legs were shaking, I was ready to tap out, but I wasn't going down that easy. I stood up sitting him down climbing on top, giving the ride of his life after riding him for about fifteen minutes straight Ty was pulling out nutting all over the place. I picked the sponge up from the shower floor and washed his body, and he washed mine. Once we finished, I dried off, getting into bed. We talked about when my kids come home how things were going to go until we fell asleep.

———

THE NEXT DAY

I FINALLY GOT IN CONTACT WITH STAR AND SKY. THEY wanted to meet with me. I had them thinking I was going to be a dancer; it was the only way I could get Onah and them in the same room. I went to warm my truck up while Onah finished getting dressed. I didn't have any makeup on, wore a pair of blue jeans and a long-sleeve black shirt with black timberlands. I wore my hair in a bun with bangs, after my meeting with Star, and Onah, I had a visit to see the kids.

I yelled. "Onah hurry the fuck up, I have other shit to do today." I walked back out to the truck, got in, and waited on Onah slow ass. I checked my cellphone for the location Star sent me. The drive would take an hour due to construction going on. I put the address into the GPS, and when Onah got into my truck, we hit the highway to Muskegon. The whole drive there was quite. I didn't want Onah to think I wanted to rebuild shit. I pulled up to a warehouse. I was starting to get a bad vibe. I called Star, but she didn't answer. I didn't see any other cars parked outside I was getting ready to pull off when an unknown number called my phone, I didn't want to answer it, but I did.

I answered it. "Hello."

I was getting ready to hang up when I heard a familiar voice that I hadn't heard in years, "Nikki?".

Nikki sounded as if she was whispering, telling me

where to find the Star and Sky, and she didn't sound normal at all. I pulled off once I got the correct address. I hit the highway driving to Kalamazoo, I wasn't into wasting time or my gas, but those hoes just tried to play me. I couldn't get to Kalamazoo fast enough. While I was driving, I called the unknown number back, and to my surprise, Nikki answered.

"Why are you helping me?" I yelled into the phone. Nikki broke everything done to me.

"I'm dying Elyte, Star and Sky are treating me like shit. They killed X, and I'm scared for my life. I don't know how much time I have left on this earth. Onah was irritating as fuck, but she didn't deserve what they did to her." Nikki confessed, hanging up the phone.

I screamed for her name, but it was too late. "Nikki!". The line went dead.

I prayed to God that Star and Sky didn't try any slick shit, or they were going to catch a bullet to the head. The drive to Sky house took forever, but we had finally pulled up on her. I parked the truck at the concern. I explained to Onah what was going to happen.

I didn't like Onah, but my bitch wasn't about to walk in a war zone without a gun. I popped my glove compartment pulled out two black .40 caliber handguns handing one to Onah.

"Look, Onah, I'll go to the front door you go to the back they won't be expecting you," I snapped at her. I knocked on the front door and Sky snatched the door open, I hit her in the face with my pistol. I hear footsteps upstairs. I opened the back door and let Onah in. As we crept up the stairs, we could hear people talking. When we made it upstairs, Brinks was sitting in a chair, counting money talking to one of his goons. I signaled Onah to check the other rooms while I handled Brinks. I walked into the room and pointed my gun at Brink's goon and sent one single shot to his head. Onah walked into the room with fire in her eyes.

"What the fuck is this Brinks," Onah shouted, aiming her gun at him.

Brinks chuckled. "Man, I don't have to explain shit to you bitches, especially you dirty little hoes," Brinks barked.

I cocked my gun. "I know you and the twins fucked Onah over. I know y'all set everything up, and my bitch is here to collect everything y'all took from her, including her money and club." I was fuming.

Sky walked ran into the room, acting like she was superwoman. Sky hit Onah, and all hell broke loose. Onah was fucking Sky up until Brinks jumped up from his desk and snatched Onah off of Sky. I waited for Onah to get back up on her feet before I did anything, she took too long for me. I did what any best friend would have done. I started stumping the shit out of Sky. I was beating Sky ass so bad she was balled up in a fetal position on the carpet crying she was pregnant as she tried to guard her stomach. I felt Brinks pull me. I snatched away from him, and I heard Onah cocked her gun and pulled the trigger. She shot and killed Sky instantly.

I stood there froze when I looked up Brinks ass was gone that pissed me off, he got away.

"Come on, Deja, before the police get here," Onah yelled. We got shit to do. I walked over Sky's dead body.

Onah asked me to pull over by the Kalamazoo River. I pulled over I watched Onah wrapped both guns up and tossed them in the Kalamazoo river before we left.

Once we finally made it back to my house, we sat in the living room talking about what our next step was going to be.

"What the fuck was that about Onah?" I asked, cutting my eye at her.

Onah looked at me with a blank face. "Them bitches took everything from me. I'm done being nice. Everything I lost. I'm taking back period."

Onah paced the floor. "Try calling Nikki again, she knows, more than what she told us," Onah demanded.

I tried calling Nikki, but she didn't answer me, I sat my phone down, and I laid my head back on the couch. I had two hours before my visit to see the kids, and I needed to clear my mind. I heard my front door slam, and I jumped up from the couch, trying to figure out what the fuck was going on. My nerves were already bad.

"Damn Onah, why are you making all that noise

slamming my fucking door?" I walk towards her cussing her out.

Onah looked at me with bloodshot red eyes.

"Deja, everything is on the line right now, including my freedom. I got shit I'm trying to do, and I don't feel like I got all your attention," Onah shouted.

"Fuck you, Onah, I see you on some other shit," I slammed my front door, leaving her out in the cold.

I looked out the window I saw Onah walk off. I saw Ty pull up to the house, and he tried to stop her, but she brushed passed him. I had to start rethinking our friendship. We were going in two different directions. I heard Ty come in the house, so I acted like I was watching the tv. He walked in, looking concerned.

"What the fuck was that about Deja," Ty muttered looking at me.

"Nothing Ty," I smacked my lips irritated.

"It was something for you two to be pissed of right now. Every time you hang with Onah you engage in hoodrat active and that shit stops today from here on out you are not to be seen or talk to Onah. A bounty is on her head, and if I find out you dealing with her it will be a problem do you understand me," Ty shouted

I scoffed at Ty demands because it pissed me off. "Are you kidding? This has to be a joke right. You don't run me nor shit in my house, nigga".

I tried to explain to Ty cutting Onah off wouldn't be that easy, but he wasn't trying to hear the shit I was saying. When Ty left back out of the house, I tried calling Onah, but she never answered me, so I left her a voicemail.

"Call me, O, we need to talk asap."

I had twenty minutes to make it to my visit to see the kids, the shit with Onah was bugging me, but I had to let it go. I wasn't going to take that bad energy in with me. Every time I saw my siblings, my heart melts. I walked into the visit feeling like a new person. While sitting in the waiting room, I got an unusual text message from an unknown number.

Unknown: *Is this Deja?*

Me: *Why, who the fuck is this?*

Unknown: *Meet me at the corner of Hall and Grandville at the car lot at 7 pm you will find out. I have some vital information you want to know.*

Me: *Word.*

After I replied to the text, the caseworker called my name. I had to push all that shit to the back of my mind. It was time for my siblings and me to vibe and catch up. I turned my cellphone off and walked into the room where our visit would take place. When I walked into the room, Dreka almost tackled me.

9

ONAH

Ever since that shit happened with Deja, I haven't seen her or talked to her. Ty acted like he was my daddy, he moved me into my apartment, and he was strict on me. He was acting funny, and that didn't sit with me too well, and I was going to get to the bottom of it. I had a trail on Star and Brinks; they were laying low in the city after Sky funeral. I had a few tricks up my sleeves; their days were number, and I was going to be the one to put them to an end. While sitting in the Restaurant, I saw Deja and her kids walk into the sprint store. I got up, excusing myself from the table. I walked upon her in the store, and she looked completely different, she was glowing. I wanted to know why she ignored me.

"Damn, bitch, you can post on Facebook and Instagram, but you can reply to my text messages. What the fuck Deja," I screamed at her because my feelings were hurt, and she needs to know I was serious with her.

Deja rolled her eyes at me like she was irritated with me. It took everything in me not to beat her ass because she had her kids with her, she was too beefy with me for no reason if anything I should be mad her ass.

"I've been busy Onah damn, you the one walked out my house and said fuck me remember" Deja snapped at me.

I always knew when Deja was lying to me, and I wasn't feeling the lie she was trying to feed me. I always did crazy shit, but I never meant it, and she knows how I can get sometimes. We stood there staring each other down like we were in a shoot-out. We were becoming distant friends, and that hurt me. I loved her like a sister, and she was treating me like shit.

"WELL, I HAVE TO GO BEFORE MY FOOD GET COLD, DEJ, you make sure you hit me up," when I turned away, I could have sworn I heard her call me a fake bitch.

I walked back across the street annoyed, Deja was acting like a bitch, and I could be an even bigger bitch. As I sat and ate my food talking to my informant, I tried to call Ty to see what he was up to, but he never answered me. I put my phone down and relaxed and enjoyed my food. I missed doing stuff like this with Deja.

I finally made it home, and Ty car was sitting parked in front of the house, which was weird and unusual for him I unlocked the door to only walk in on him packing his clothes I couldn't speak, I was lost on what was going on.

"Why are you packing Tyrek? Where are you going," I hit him with question after question, but he never replied to me.

He moved around the house like a thief in the night taking all of his belongings. He had stop packing and asked for me to have a seat. Shit, I knew we were having problems, but no, this big for him to move up out the fucking house.

"What the fuck Ty, you skipping out on me?" I asked with tears in my eyes and a frog in my throat. I hated when my feelings got hurt because I turned into a bold ass bitch, and I was trying my hardest not to at this moment.

"Look, we haven't been happy in weeks Onah, you care more about your revenge, you haven't paid any attention to me. You always on a steak out looking for trouble, you don't show a nigga no type of attention, and I'm tired of it", Ty explained, getting up from the couch.

I couldn't help it. I broke down crying. I knew getting back involved with him was stupid.

"I'm sorry, I'm just trying to clear my muthafuckin name and get my shit back, I lost a lot of shit behind Brinks, I trusted him and if you dint understand that then yeah get the fuck out and go back to Deja," I snapped feeling the tears come down my face.

Tyrek grabbed his bags and headed for the front door, everything in me wanted to go after him, but my pride wouldn't let me. My mom wasn't shit, but she told me never to run after a man after he dogs you out. I wish my mom were here for moments like this I'll have a shoulder to cry on. After Ty left, I sat in my bedroom, drinking a whole bottle of wine with a double shot of Henny mixed. I needed and wanted to numb the hurt feeling. I called Deja, and to my surprise, she answered the phone.

"Hey girl," Deja's voice echoed through the phone.

"Hey, Deja, can you talk right now?" I whispered like someone was listening to me.

"Yeah, I got the time right now, the kids taking a nap," Deja stated.

"My man left me, he said I was boring, and he needed something a little bit more for him. I'm hurt, and I'm pissed off a couple of months down the drain because I was obsessed with getting the muthafuckas who took everything from me," I sobbed uncontrollably.

For the first time, Deja didn't have anything to say, and she always had a mouth full spitting out. I hung up on her slow ass. I was starting to feel drunk, so I laid on my couch with Pandora blasting through the house. Here it was a Friday night, and I was in the house crying over a nigga who didn't deserve me. I had fallen asleep with the wine bottle in my lap. When I woke up in the middle of the night, I heard a glass break, and I jumped up from the couch, still drunk, I pulled my gun out my purse.

"Who the fuck in my house," I yelled, ready to air the bitch out. I heard footsteps getting closer, and I started firing my gun. When I made it my kitchen, my back door was wide open, I grabbed my phone and calling the police.

When the police got there, I was holding my stomach. I was cramping really badly, and I couldn't stop throwing up. That shit scared me to the point I made myself sick. The police had the fluorescence van come take pictures. I left my house. I was still feeling like shit, so I decided to go to urgent care I was coming down with a cold I felt it. I found out I was eight weeks pregnant, and I knew Ty was the father. The time I conceived puts me back to the night, we slept together at Deja's house.

After finding out I was pregnant, my whole world came crashing down. I tried hitting Ty up, but he was ignoring me. I gave up on contacting him. I didn't need a kid right now, not with the shit I had going on. I made my mind up I was going to get an abortion next week, and I didn't care if Ty found out or not my mind was made up. The morning sickness was killing me. I couldn't keep my head out of the toilet or trash can this baby had to go. I had lost so much weight because I was always throwing up. I called Deja the next day to see if she'll go with me next week to the clinic her phone rang four times before she picked up and when she did, I could have sworn I heard Ty voice in the background.

"Hey, Deja, I know it's early, but I need you," I started sobbing. I couldn't hold it in any longer.

"What's up, Onah," Deja spoke into the sounding out of breath.

"I'm getting an abortion next Friday it would mean a lot to me if you came to support me. You don't have to give me an answer right now, but please give me one before next Friday," I hung the phone up and laid back down in my bed the room was spinning.

"Don't you think the dad should know what you are doing?" Deja suggested on the other end of the phone.

"Fuck him Dej, I been trying to contact him all night, and this morning he still hasn't picked up the fucking phone, not to mention someone broke in my house last night," I smacked my lips I was annoyed with the whole situation.

I was bugging out. I thought I heard Ty voice in Deja's background. I almost wrecked my brain thinking of different scenarios of why he would even be over there. I ended the phone call and went to sleep. I woke back up about noon feeling even sicker. I got ill just at the sight of seeing him made me sick," I rolled my eyes getting up from my vanity walking into the bathroom.

"What are you doing here, Ty I didn't tell you to come over," I told in a stern voice already irritated and sick.

"I heard you were pregnant and trying to kill my seed," Ty's voice cracked.

When those words left his mouth, I knew Deja had opened her fucking mouth. I knew she was going to be sick when she found out I was pregnant with Ty's baby. Pissed off was an understatement. I was furious. I was ready to kill her ass even though she didn't think he was the dad she had no business I knew. I knew I wasn't tripping when I heard his voice in her background.

"Are you serious Ty," I scoffed. You broke up with me because I was trying to take back what was mine in the first place. Don't think you can come up in here questioning me about my body? I don't think so nigga," I picked up the Bluetooth speaker sitting on my nightstand by the bed, and threw it at him, but he moved just in time, and the speaker hit the wall.

"What the fuck Onah you tripping," Ty shouted.

I walked right passed Ty and headed downstairs, I had that sick feeling again, and I knew I was getting ready to vomit. Before I made it the bottom of the steps, I was throwing up all over myself and stairs. I notice Ty was standing over me trying to pull my hair back, but I pushed his hands away from me." Don't touch me," I was upset I was going to miss my meeting to find out where Star was. I couldn't go being this fucking sick Ty kept asking me questions, I was ready for him to leave my house and leave me alone but he followed me to the bathroom.

"Onah, you need to talk to me. This is both of our baby, and I don't need you making a dumb ass decision you won't be able to take back," Ty yelled at me, but I wasn't trying to hear him.

"I'm not talking to you about my body Ty you lost that privilege when you dumped me," I stopped throwing up and made my way to the bathroom. I needed a shower and to clean my steps.

When I got out of the shower, I smelled Pine-sol. When I walked to the stairs, Ty was cleaning up my mess. I felt bad. I went to my room and got dressed. Once I was done, I made my way back downstairs. I stopped Tyrek from cleaning.

"I got this. You need to go," I mumbled then took the mop out his hands.

Tyrek gave me a blank stare. "Seriously, Onah. Bet."

"You need to leave my house and don't ever come back," I snatched the mop from his hands.

I folded my arms across my chest and slid down until I reached the steps. I was in my feelings and probably overthinking shit, but Ty needed t know he had to pick between Deja and me.

Once I heard the front door slam, I finished cleaning the stairs. Once I did that, I took the mop bucket to the kitchen and poured out the dirty water, then rinsed my mop out. I went and laid down on my couch. While flipping through the channels, Deja called me, asking if I wanted to go to Brandon's party at the Shells Room, and I accepted her open invitation. I took me a much-needed three-hour nap. After I woke up, I notice the wad of cash sitting on my coffee table Ty must have put that there on the table when I was in the shower. I took it, and I headed to the mall to get myself a cute outfit. I went to Windsor and Charming Charlie's. I walked around and shopped until I couldn't shop anymore. I hit my hairstylist Tone up to see if she could install my lace front and bundles today once she told me she could fit me in, I was happy I drove to her hair salon happy as hell. I was about to be on fleek. Once my hair was finished, I left. I went to Deja's to get ready when I pulled up. I saw Ty and Deja standing on her porch, arguing, which was not normal at all.

"Hey Ty," I waved when I walked up the steps heading into Deja's house.

I walked in and sat my bags on her couch. I noticed Deja had moved her whole house around since the last time I was over. It was quiet, so I had to ask her where they were.

"Girl, where the kids at?" I asked, looking around the house.

Deja started smiling hard. "They didn't want to come until Saturday. They are at a sleepover at a friend's house, and this was my chance to link back up with you."

"Oh, okay. What's going on with you and Ty, I saw

y'all looked like y'all was in a heated argument or something,

"Can I ask you something Deja without you getting mad at me. Are you really happy with Tyrek?"

I broke down crying this pregnancy was making me too emotional, and I hated myself for it because I felt so weak. I didn't know I could feel like this about a nigga

"I'm not mad at all. We have our days but were okay. Now go get dressed before we are late," Deja walked off, leaving me standing in the living room.

After spending almost two hours getting ready, we were finally ready to hit the "Greenlight" club, it was the hottest club in Grand Rapids, and I was feeling alive. I wasn't feeling sick, which was a good thing. I took a shot of Cîroc and lit my blunt up. I was trying to loosen up. When we arrived at Deja's friend's party, it was lit. I was happy we were on the VIP list because it was freezing outside, standing outside was a no go for me. Once we made it inside the club, all eyes were on us, my bitch, and I always cleaned up nice when we hit the City. We made it to the VIP rope, and Deja's friend met us and told the bouncer to let us through. The fellas in VIP looked dehydrated. They were extra thirsty tonight. I poured myself some Grey Goose and cranberry juice in my cup. I sat back watching the scene when my eyes landed on Ty's ugly ass he was sitting at the bar with his boys. I was so deep in my thoughts; I didn't notice the man who sat next to me until he tapped me on the shoulder.

"Umm do I know you," I frowned at him

"Nah, but I'm hoping to get to know you baby girl," when the strange man whispered in my ear, he sent chills down my spine, and that hasn't happened in a long time.

Deja and I were turn't up with her friends in VIP when *Cardi B "Be Careful"* came blaring through the club, and I was feeling my liquor. My new male friend I had just met watched my every move. I notice Ty was sitting at the bar with his boys looking up at us. My pettiness had kicked into overdrive. I stood up walked to the balcony I grabbed the rail and proceeded to slow dance to the beat of *"Be Careful"* I rapped every word to Ty bitch ass. I felt a pair of hands on my hips, and I didn't bother to look back. I was feeling myself, and I know Ty felt it. He stared daggers into my soul, but I ignored him. I closed my eyes when I opened them Ty was gone. Deja tapped me, letting me know Ty and his niggas were on there, way up, but I didn't give a fuck. I sat back down, talked to my friend I had met when I saw Ty snatch Deja up from the couch. I heard her yelling.

"Put me the fuck down," Deja screamed at the top of her lungs, trying to fight Ty ass. I was tired of him thinking he ran both or our lives. He could do what he wanted to do, but we couldn't. That shit ended when he broke up with me.

Ty carried Deja out of the club like she was Jane, and he was Tarzan. I guess he got tired of her yelling and punching him in the back. He dropped her on the cement. She looked embarrassed it was so many people outside looking at us. I was on their heels when I saw Ty drop Deja. I went into beast mood, ready to fuck him up.

"Onah, if you don't get the fuck in the car, you will be stranded," Ty barked, pushing Deja in the car, slamming the door.

I open the back door and got in slamming it almost breaking the window Deja was going the fuck off on Ty.

"Why the fuck you snatching me out of clubs and I'm not your bitch Ty you broke up with me earlier I'm tired of you thinking you run me nigga because you don't own me fuck y...," Ty, smacked Deja so hard in the face I saw stars for her.

All the pent-up anger I had inside of me started to come out. I sat back in the backseat, ready to beat his ass in the face. I sat back, and looking through my Instagram, I was trying to avoid eye contact with Ty. I was feeling uncomfortable. It was a Friday night, and I was going to be in the house before 2 am.

When I woke up it was almost 7 in the morning when I looked up Ty ass was standing over me looking crazy. It scared the shit out of my mind.

"Boy, what the fuck wrong with you standing over

me in the fucking dark. You almost gave me a heart attack," I ranted, sitting up in the bed.

I turned on the lamp sitting on the nightstand. I noticed Ty was shirtless, and in his pajama's pants, his chocolate skin was glowing. I was ready to take a bit out of his sexy ass. I saw his dick was semi-hard. I reached my hands inside his pants, stroked his dick, then dropped to my knees. The sounds of his moans escaping his lips turned me on. I wrapped my warm lips around his thick mushroom tip. I took him into my mouth, giving the sloppiest head he had ever had in his life. I could have sworn I heard his toes crack. Ty stepped back, gripping my hair thrusting harder into my mouth, almost making me gag, but I open my mouth wider, giving him the access so he could go to work.

"Whoa wait a minute now, Onah, you about to make a nigga bust I want to hit that. Bend that ass over," Ty demanded man handing me turning me on even more.

I climbed onto the bed, put my ass in the air before I could tell him to put on a condom, he slid inside of me from the back. With every stroke he delivered. I was falling more in love with my best friend's nigga. Ty was making so much noise I almost forgot we were in Deja's house.

"Ssshhhh, you are going to wake Deja up," I flipped on my back, giving him full access to my freshly shaved wet pussy, and I needed him to look me in my eyes.

"I love you, Ty," The words slipped out of my mouth so smooth I couldn't believe what I just said.

Ty made me get on top. I climbed on him, catching my rhythm. I was ready to cum as I felt the chills creep up my spine.

"I'm about to cum Ty, please don't stop," I smothered my face into the pillow so it could muffle my moans as I came collapsing onto his chest.

Ty gripped my ass thrusting inside of me, and I couldn't take it any longer, I begged him to stop almost in tears.

I shouted at the top of my lung. "Okay, okay, please stop." Ty smacked me on my ass, nutting in me. I jumped up fast as fuck snapping on.

"Why, would you do that dumb shit, Ty. I told you not to nut in me," I stood there looking at him.

"Chill out Onah, you already pregnant," Ty put back on his pajama pants the walked out the room.

The next morning, I woke up I was sick as hell throwing up, I got dressed and went to CVS on Eastern and 28 street. I walked up and down the aisle trying to find some medicine to stop the morning sickness, but I couldn't find anything, I was close to saying fuck it and walk out until a female pharmacy tech helped me out. I rushed back to Deja's house so I could take the nausea medicine and chill out for the rest of the day. When I walked into the house, I noticed the kids were there. It was super early; it was almost 8:30 am. I thought her drunk ass would still be sleep. I walked right passed them heading to my room as I was getting ready to open the pill it was a knock at the door.

Knock. Knock

"What," I yelled, snatching the door open seeing it was Deja instead of Ty.

"Damn, bitch who pissed in your frosting flakes this morning," Deja folded her arms, looking right into the room. I tried to close the door, but she busted into the room on me.

"Who did you get knocked up by Onah?".

I dropped my head. "I met up with an old boo-thang, and shit got a little crazy, and now it's this," I lied right through my teeth, not even caring.

A COUPLE OF HOURS LATER

I was in a deep sleep when I heard the doorbell was ringing, I tried to ignore the sound but whoever it was wasn't letting up. I got up pissed off. It was almost ten in the morning, and the sun was shining bright.

"Who is it?".

When I opened the door, I almost grabbed the metal bat, getting ready to knock whoever head off their shoulder.

"What the fuck are you doing here on my steps Star, I should kill you right now and how the fuck did you find me, bitch," I yelled, gripping the bat ready to swing.

"I'm not here to fight Onah. I just lost my sister. I'm here to bring peace. We need to come up with some type of mutual agreement. By the way, you saw Brinks. I know you been looking for us, and he's now missing and word on the street you fucking your best friends' man. I wonder how Deja would feel if she found out about you two?" Star growled, jumping up in my face.

I scoffed. "You have to be kidding me, right? I don't know where the fuck you got your information from, but if you must know, I'm still looking for Brink broke ass myself. You don't know what the fuck you're talking about. Wherever you got your information got you all fucked up, I advise you to stay in your lane and get the fuck off Deja porch before your mom buries you next".

Star roughed a couple of feathers with that bombshell she dropped on me, and I had to make sure Deja didn't find out. I had to get in contact with Ty as soon as possible. I ran me a nice hot bubble bath dropping a bath bomb into my water. I close my eyes and slid under the water, trying to wash the night away. When I opened my eyes, Ty was standing over me once more I came up for air coughing because water got in my nose and mouth.

"Boy, make some damn noise next time, you almost gave me a heart attack," I reached for my towel so I can dry my face off, but he snatched it away from me.

Ty sat on the toilet, looking at me, and I didn't like the vibe he was giving me.

"Why are you looking at me like that Ty,"

"Last night I think you may have been a little too drunk, do you remember what happened?" Ty asked, throwing my drying towel on the floor.

"Yes," I whispered in a low tone.

"Since you know I don't need to waste my time explaining why Deja can't find out about us," Ty expressed then walked out the bathroom, leaving me there to think about what he wanted to talk about.

I dried off and put on a sweat suit meeting him in the living room. I was too nervous about speaking up about the shit Star told me. Ty sat in the loveseat sweating bullets. I could say to the suspense was killing him. I sat on the couch, waiting on him to start talking.

"What's so important, Onah? " Ty sat back, watching my every move.

"Star popped up at the house about an hour two ago basically telling me the streets are talking about us messing around, I so badly wanted to take her fucking head off, but I didn't want to bring the heat to Deja's house. I told her she didn't know what the fuck she was talking about," I groaned.

Ty sat there quit which scared me because I didn't know what he was thinking. He put his head down as if he was stressed out. "So, what we go do about this."

I almost fell over when he said that. What he said caught me way off guard, and I felt like dying at that exact moment, or I wanted to go into hiding. I was scared Deja was going to find out, and if she did, I knew shit was going to be ugly. I stood up, trying to think of a plan and fast.

"Figure it out, Onah, if you kill her, you can have me all to yourself," Ty stood up, walked towards me, backing me into the corner in the living room.

I cleared my throat, speaking. "You want me to do what? Boy, you smoking that good dope," I stated.

He hovered over me, kissing me, I was getting ready to fuck him in Deja living room. I hated I let myself get caught under his spell. I couldn't resist him. He pulled my pants down, rubbed on my clit. His touches were driving me crazy. Once I felt him slip, I finger in me I knew it was about to get real nasty. Tyrek pulled out his dick, picking me up pushing me against the wall he was going to town on my ass I heard the garage door open.

"Wait, I think Deja here," I tapped Ty on the shoulders he was deep off into fucking that he didn't hear it.

He put me down, and I ran to my room, fixing myself, acting like I was sleep. When I heard the door open, I acted like I was sleep praying to God that Deja didn't suspect a thing. I listened to the kids talking and laughing, through me off why Ty was in there acting like he just wasn't fucking me that shit pissed me off.

I heard Deja yell. "It's food out here if you're hungry." I laid there until I didn't hear them in the kitchen anymore. The shit Tyrek asked me to do made me somewhat sick to my stomach I couldn't do Deja like that.

10

DEJA

I woke up to Ty gone in the middle of the night it looked like he never came to be I didn't think anything of it, so I went back to sleep. My head was still pounding, we got into it at the club because got jealous and cut up. I had to be up early because the kids were coming to spend the night, and I had our whole day planned out. I looked around the house looking for Ty, and he was nowhere to be found. I walked into the kitchen, making a pop of coffee so I could wake up. I sat on the couch listening to the Steve Harvey morning show strawberry letter, and it caught my attention, almost making me spit my coffee out. The letter was title *"transgender woman."* her husband wanted kids, but she couldn't have any, and she didn't know how to tell. As Steve gave her advice, my doorbell rang, and I cut off the radio, opened the door. When I opened the door, the kids attack me, almost knocking me over.

"Deja." They yelled, hugging me and smiling ear to ear.

I was almost in tears. "I missed y'all too.

We sat in the living room, talking and catching up. I then realized I was always meant to take care of them. If ain't nobody had them, I know I did. My baby sister was almost thirteen-years old looking just like our mother, and Zayden and Zyier were handsome. They were a year apart eight and seven. We didn't know who their dads were because my mom was wild and reckless back then. I showed them their new rooms so they could get settled and comfortable with their rooms. An hour later, they were hungry; we were getting ready to walk out the door when Onah almost knocked us over, rushing in the house. I didn't say anything to her in front of the kids. I watched her speed walk until she disappeared. I heard her tussling in her room when I knocked on the door, she snatched it open like she was annoyed by my presents, but it didn't bother because she was at my house. When she opened the door, I saw nauseous medication on the bed, and she looked stressed out.

"Onah, I was just coming to check on you," I stood there trying to read her, but I couldn't pick up on shit at the moment.

After she told me she was fine, I took the kids to an all you can eat buffet at the *Gold Corral* on Alpine. We stuffed our faces until we couldn't stuff them anymore. Once we were done eating, I took the kids to Jimmy Jazz to get some shoes and to get the boy's haircut. Zayden was crying because he was tired. I stopped and picked up dinner before heading home. I noticed Dreka was looking at me while I was driving.

"What's on your mind, baby girl?" I pulled into the New York Fried Chicken. I looked in the backseat, and both boys were asleep.

"I'm just happy to hang out with my big sister. That's all," Dreka chuckled.

The rest of the ride home was quite the food had the whole truck smelling good. As I was pulled up, I noticed Tyrek's ass was finally at home. I had a lot of shit on my mind, and him going MIA pissed me off most.

Dreka asked. "Is that the lucky man my sister is crazy about."

"Yes, it is let's go meet him," I opened the garage and killed the engine. I grabbed the food, and Dreka woke Zayden and Zyier up. When I walked into the house, it smelled funny. I sat the food on the dining room table and looked for Ty.

"Come here, Tyrek," I beamed with excitement at the bottom of the stairs.

Tyrek's whole vibe was off, and I didn't like it at all. He had been acting funny for a little minute now, and it was pissing me off. After I introduce the kids, we ate, and they went to their rooms to relax. I tried to take Onah food, but she was still sleeping, which was weird.

As I was sitting there eating the same unknown number text me.

Unknown: *Meet me at woody's on 54th street in forty-five minutes I think it time you find out who I am*

Me: *I'll be there.*

I was tired of this person harassing me, and it stopped today. I cleaned my mess up, putting on my coat.

"Where are you going, Deja," Tyrek asked.

"I'm going out for a while. The kids are in their rooms. They won't bother you. I'll be back," I walked out of the house.

The whole drive there, I thought, what if I get kidnapped or killed, but I took a chance this person was too interested in me. When I pulled up, I didn't see anyone in the parking lot. I sat there waiting almost an hour when a black SUV whipped in the parking lot, I hit the locks on my door and grabbed my gun from underneath my seat. The two men jumped out, walked up to my truck. I was getting ready to start shooting when the man removed his cap, asking me to roll the window down.

"I'm not here to hurt you, sweetheart, this is for you," The man handed me a yellow envelope. I looked at him, lost.

"What's this?". I opened the envelope, and pictures of Tyrek and Onah fell out they were dated back to 2013, and they looked more to be together than just friends. I looked through every photo, and two of them caught my eyes. Tyrek was hugged up with Onah taking her shopping. My blood was started to boil, and I was ready to shoot everybody.

"Why are you showing me this," I tried to fight the tears back, but I couldn't my best friend and man had been playing me this whole time.

"Message from the boss man," the big black man walked off opened the back door of the truck I got out walked to the truck when I saw X-rated, I almost passed out. It had been years since I saw him, and I knew this meeting was going to go so well.

X-rated looked a lot different now, he was missing an eye, and he lost a lot of weight. I was scared because he was not to be fucked it.

"Why you call this meeting with me out of all people X?" I mumbled.

X cleared his throat. "I'm here offering you a peace offering, I know you and Onah killed Sky, and y'all took out one of my best men. I could kill you now, but I don't want you, Deja, I want Onah. She took a lot of money from me, I had to make it seem like I was dead, but Brinks stepped in watching her every move".

When X called me by my name, my heart dropped. "But how do you know this is real?" I asked.

"I know about all my girls that work for me. I hired you because you were different, and I needed that in my club. You would be surprised how dirty bitches are," X cracked his window, lighting his Cuban cigar smoke out.

I took in every word he was saying, but it wasn't making any sense to.

"So, what are you saying, X?".

"I'm saying everything that happened to Onah was because of me, and she owes me her fucking life," X hit the seat scaring me.

I was starting to feel very uncomfortable, but I was mad at the same time, Onah been playing me the whole time.

X put his cigar out grunting. "Look, she been sleeping with your man and playing you and him. They have been working together if you don't see that I feel sorry for you. I'm going to give you my number I'm trying to set something up, but it's going to take some time are you down to get rid of this bitch Onah once and for all?".

I shook my head. "Yes."

I took X number and exited the truck feeling stupid I was yet again played by Onah but for Tyrek to play her sick ass game. I drove home, sobbing. I had to pull over and get my shit together I was hurt and betrayed Onah was a grimy bitch. I made it back, and the kids were in the living room watching tv with Ty and Onah. I went to my room so I could think of my plan to get rid of both of their asses. I text X number, letting him know I was down, but I wanted to be the one to pull the trigger on Onah hoe ass.

11

ONAH

THREE MONTHS LATER

Deja called me to hang out a couple of times since, but my stomach was noticeable. I was almost four months pregnant, and Tyrek treated me like shit, he was beating my ass and cheating on me. I was paranoid I felt like muthafuckas we're following me. I was lying down in bed when I heard shots ring out, my bedroom window shattered, and I dropped to the floor. I covered my stomach screaming. I felt the warm liquid coming down my leg, and I noticed I was hit. I crawled to my phone and called Ty to tell him what had just happened he told me to stay put, but I didn't have it. I heard the sirens coming. When I looked down, I noticed my leg was cut. I took my head-scarf off my head and wrapped my leg and got out of the house. I went out the back door, scared for my life. I got in my car, pulling out of the driveway in time. I called Deja scared out my mind; my stomach was starting to hurt.

I pulled up to Deja's house, and she and her little sister Dreka were sitting on the porch playing Uno. I sat there for a few, I saw Deja walk towards my car, and I popped the locks, letting her in.

"What the fuck Onah, why you are bringing this type of bullshit to my doorstep, and the kids are home bitch," Deja snapped on me to the point I started crying. I tried to use my shirt to dry my tears, revealing my stomach.

"So, you're keeping the baby who's the dad for real? Because I don't believe your little fling story."

Deja was asking so many questions that I was starting to regret showing up at her house.

"I am, and my baby daddy got himself into some shit, and now the muthafuckas found out where I stayed and shot my apartment up, hitting me in the arm. I'm too scared to go to the Spectrum health I need for you to help me, please. I plan to leave Michigan before my baby daddy finds his enemies or me," I lied.

Deja got out the car helped me out the car, and we went into her house. She took me into her bathroom, pulled a first aid kit from under the sink. I sat there watching her get towels and a needled and thread from her mirror. She stuck a rag in my mouth, telling me.

"This is going to hurt Onah, do you trust me?".

I looked at her with tears in my eyes, shaking my head. "Yes." I closed my arms soon as she unwrapped my arm, and I passed out it was too much blood for me to handle. I woke up to a cold rag on my head. I felt like shit when I woke up. I was putting Deja in another fucked up ass situation. As she was stitching me up, I passed out again, and when I woke back up, I was in Deja's bed. I tried to get out of the bed, but my body was sore, I laid there, and for the first time I felt my baby moved I wanted to cry and smile at the same time. I hated this pregnancy made me so messed up. I looked around for my phone, and I couldn't find it. I called for Deja when she walked into the room. She looked like she had been crying. Her eyes were puffy and red.

"Can you see if I left my phone it the car my baby daddy probably tried to call me by now," I rolled over on my side, waiting for her to return.

I heard footsteps coming up the stairs I figure it was Deja until I listened to the familiar voice that made me sit up in the bed.

"Hello, Onah, you missed me."

When I looked up, it was X. I pissed on myself and passed out when I woke up, I was in a dark trunk with my hands tied behind my back the car was moving. I screamed for Deja, but she never answered me. The dive was so long I ended up falling asleep when the car finally stopped, I woke up. When the truck open, I felt like my heart stopped; Brinks was snatching me out the truck throwing me over his shoulder, taking me into a dark warehouse. I was put into a dark room I tried screaming, but that didn't help.

"Help me. Help me...Help".

Brinks walked into the room and punched me in the face. "Shut up, bitch, don't scream now." Those were the last words I heard before blocking out.

12

DEJA

Onah had me fucked upcoming to my house with her drama. Once X let me know the plan was in motion, I took her in acting as I cared. Once she told me the sad sob story about her baby daddy. I was ready to drive the scissors through her heart, but I didn't want to ruin the plan because I was killing her ass. When they snatched Ty dog ass up, I let my siblings go with their foster parents for the week since summer was getting ready to end. I followed X to Wayland until we got on a dirt road. I popped my truck getting out, I had drugged Tyrek bitch ass and put him the truck, he was still sleeping like a fucking baby. The warehouse looked rundown and dirty.

"Damn, girl, I didn't know you had it in you," Brinks yelled as he dragged Ty into the warehouse. The windows were boarded up. All of X workers were standing around smoking and shooting dice. I saw Star squatting on the floor playing dice she grabbed her money and got up from the floor

"You sure you ready to do this, Deja, you won't be able to back out of this once you step in that room," Star stated, looking at me. I walked into the lion den I probably wasn't going to make it out alive, but Onah and Ty were going to get their karma. I turned on the lights then walked into the room with Star, Brinks, and X on my heels. Onah was sitting in the chair trying to loosen her hands, but they were tied behind her back when she saw me her eyes grew big.

"Oh, don't be scared now, you grimy little bitch," I snapped, taking my jacket off.

Onah tried to scream, but a rag was in her mouth, I had a devilish grin on my face and that shit I know it sent chills up her spine. When they brought Ty into the room, he was bleeding from his nose and his mouth. He was unconscious. They tied him to a chair right beside Onah.

"What the fuck is this Deja you flipped on me for these pussy niggas?" Onah sobbed, looking at X and Brinks.

I was on some sinter shit. I didn't take shit easy when my feelings got hurt, but I never thought my own best friend would stoop that low. Onah was staring at me a little bit too hard. I kicked her right in the stomach she cried out in pain, trying to hold her stomach. I didn't give a fuck that she was pregnant. She did the fucking unthinkable, and for that, she and her child were going to pay for it. I walked out of the room with X and Brinks following me. I was officially done with Onah backstabbing ass. I pulled my gun from behind her back, pacing the floor. I needed answers and quick to why they would play me out of all people.

I walked back into the room, and Onah was still crying. "I'm curious to know why the both of you muthafuckas thought y'all could play me and get away with it," I stated. X picked up a crowbar and hit Ty in the chest with it, causing him to wake up coughing up blood.

I left Onah and Tyrek to think about the dumb shit they did and got me involved in. I was getting ready to leave the warehouse when X asked me what I wanted to do. I told him not to touch them until I got back in the building, I needed to smoke to clear my mind so much shit was running through my head. I was dressed in all black with gloves on I hit my cigarette a few times walking back into the building.

I yelled. "Somebody get me some hot ass water. I'm about to wake this bitch ass nigga the fuck up".

Once I got the water, I threw it ,a bucket of steaming hot water on Ty causing him to wake up yelling

"Now that I have y'all undivided attention, let's get to it," I clapped my hands together.

"How long have y'all known each other and fuck-ing?" I blurted out.

Onah nor Ty answered "Wha................. Before they could get the words out, I had shot Ty in his kneecaps. His screams were muffled due to the gage ball in his mouth. Blood was pouring out fast.

"Now, let me ask another question and somebody better answer correctly or its lights out," I demanded, sitting in a wooden chair right in front of them.

"Ty, did you know who I was?" I asked, spilling all the beans.

Ty tried to look at me with one swollen eye shut. "Yes," he mustered to get out before chocking on his blood.

"Remove this hoe ass nigga gage," I looked at Star shouting since she was standing there looking stuck on stupid.

Ty tried to clear his throat. "It wasn't supposed to be like this, I was supposed to fuck you and forget you, but I ended up falling for you," Ty confessed.

X walked into the room with a black suitcase in his hands. He handed it to me and walked back out of the room. When I opened it, I pulled out all types of different shapes and sizes of knives. I walked up to Ty and stabbed him several times in the stomach. I felt like I was in a horror movie, but I was the murder. Love could make you do some crazy shit because I had lost every emotion in my body to feel for him or Onah.

I looked at Onah, telling her not to worry Ty wasn't

dead just yet. He was hanging on by a thread as his breathing slowed down.

"Deja, you are killing him, the hate your feeling is towards me take it out on me please," Onah yelped.

Onah watched me take my gloves off and headed back out of the room. The death look Onah was giving me didn't bother as much as I bothered her. I could hear her talking to Ty I wasn't even mad because they were going to die together.

"It's going to be okay, Ty, I will get us out alive," Onah spoke softly as I walked back into the room.

I turned around and looked at Onah. Try to comfort Ty only pissed me off, even more. I walked up to her, punched her in the face Onah cried out in pain, but I didn't care.

I yelled, fell into the table, and grabbed my throat, falling to the ground. "You, bitch, you stabbed me in the stomach!".

Onah finally made it to her feet, stood over me, looking as if she had won the fight. "Deja, after all this time, I still keep a couple tricks up my sleeve." Onah laughed.

I cocked my head to the side, feeling the rage in me. "You used me this whole time. I was never your friend. You used my situation as a pawn. Every time I tried to leave and better myself, you threaten to expose that I was gay. That shit cut me deep every time, and I let I go because I felt like I needed you to survive, but now I see it was the other way around bitch." I looked around the room at everyone, including Tyrek.

"Fuck you, Deja, you ain't shit, and you will never be what I am!" Onah spit blood at my feet. She was beaten up pretty badly.

I smirked and folded my arms across my chest. "And what's that bitch. bitter?"

Onah closed her eyes and sat there like she was contemplating on what to say. "A real bitch, your past will forever haunt you, Deja. Your momma ain't shit but a recovering addict. You'll be just like her," Onah spat.

"Bitch, you're the scum on the bottom of my shoes. How am I not shit? Please say the grimy bitch you tried to paly me."

"It's funny. You say that because you're the same bootlicker ass bitch that was boosting and stripping.

"Since you have a point to prove, then prove it. If you beat my ass, I'll let you walk away, but if you don't, I promise you Onah, you'll regret the bitch I've become," I told her then stepped back.

Onah jumped and tackled me. We both hit the floor, fighting each other. I made X, and his boys leave the beef I had with Onah was between us. I won't lie Onah got some good licks in before I went into beast mood and flipped her ass. Once I had Onah pinned down, I sat on top of her punching her repeatedly until she lost consciousness, and X pulled me off of her.

"That's enough, Deja! The bitch is dead."

I snatched away from X and got off of Onah. I checked her breathing, and it was faint. I got up and dusted my hands off on my pants.

"Put her ass in the backseat I got a plan for her ass," I demanded, and X and his brothers did what I said. Once Onah unconscious body was in the backseat X, and I got into his truck. X looked over at me.

"What we about to do with this bitch?" he asked and started his truck up.

I made sure my seatbelt was on. "Take her ass to the next county and drop her ass off on the side of the road."

X pulled off, and I could hear Onah moaning and groaning in pain. We hit 131 south towards Kalamazoo, Michigan. X had to be doing 80 mph. I looked back to check on Onah, and she was still out. I turned back to watch the road, and all hell broke loose. Onah woke up and put me in a headlock, and X swerved into other lanes.

"Bitch, if I can't have Tyrek, we both might as well die together," Onah let my neck go and grabbed X's arms, and we smacked into the concrete wall and flipped over a couple of time, Onah went flying out the windshield. The airbag knocked X out. I saw Onah body lying in the middle of the road a few feet away. I popped my seatbelt and slid out of the truck. Traffic had stopped on both sides of the road. I went to check her pulse, but she didn't have one. I felt the tears running down my face. I was moving too fast. I felt weak a little. I heard the sirens in the distance, but I passed out.

A couple of weeks later, I woke up in the hospital when I looked up, my mother was standing over me, and I thought I saw shit until I heard Dreka and the kids voice. I tried talking, but something was in my throat. I started chocking. The nurses and doctors ran into the room, putting everyone out. A couple of hours late, I was sitting up in the with a sore throat and my neck bandaged up. I tried to talk, but my mother stopped me.

"You were involved in a kidnapping, and Onah and her friend didn't make it," I sat there hearing my mother, but the words weren't coming out. Brinks and X walked into the room, and my mother left. I dropped my head feeling defeated.

"Lift your head, Elyte. You did what you had to do. It was eventually going to happen," Brinks stated, pulling a chair up to my bed.

I listened to everything he and X told me, and I was shocked to find out Brinks was my daddy and every party Onah booked, he took the money, putting it to the side for me because he knew Onah was a snake. After finding out Brinks was my dad, I was lost for words. No wonder why he was always on my head when I did dumb shit. Once my mother confirmed he was my dad, everything from that day changed. I tore down the Foxxy kitten and built a hair salon hiring all the dopiest stylists and nail techs. I was going to open up a daycare for low-income families. One thing I learned about Onah she was never really my friend, but she played her part to the T.

I couldn't understand why I was crying, especially over a bitch who did me grimy.

The end